INVISIBLE HANDS

INVISIBLE HANDS

A NOVEL

Stig Sæterbakken

Translated by
Seán Kinsella

DALKEY ARCHIVE PRESS

Originally published in Norwegian as *Usynlige hender* in 2007.
Copyright © 2007 Cappelen Damm AS
Translation copyright © 2016 Seán Kinsella

First edition, 2016
All rights reserved

Library of Congress Cataloging-in-Publication Data

Names: Sæterbakken, Stig, 1966–2012, author. | Kinsella, Seán (Translator) translator.
Title: Invisible hands / by Stig Sæterbakken ; translated by Seán Kinsella.
Other titles: Usynlige hender. English
Description: First edition. | Victoria, TX : Dalkey Archive Press, 2016. | Series: Norwegian literature series
Identifiers: LCCN 2015044153 | ISBN 9781564788566 (pbk. : acid-free paper)
Subjects: LCSH: Missing persons--Fiction. | Suspense fiction.
Classification: LCC PT8951.29.A39 U8513 2016 | DDC 839.82/374--dc23
LC record available at http://lccn.loc.gov/2015044

Partially funded by the Norwegian Ministry of Foreign Affairs, and by a grant by the Illinois Arts Council, a state agency.

This translation has been published with the financial support of NORLA.

Dalkey Archive Press publications are, in part, made possible through the support of the University of Houston-Victoria and its program in creative writing, publishing, and translation.

Dalkey Archive Press
Victoria, TX / McLean, IL / London / Dublin

Cover: Art by Katherine O'Shea

www.dalkeyarchive.com

Printed on permanent/durable acid-free paper

INVISIBLE HANDS

1

I'd known since the previous day that I had to visit her, the mother of the missing child. Still, I was reluctant to do so and put it off as long as I could. Filth floated by, a river of excrement had been created by the melting snow and sent meandering down the streets. The wind picked up, people walked as though on the deck of a listing ship. I was standing under the awning by a newsstand. I'd purchased a paper, mostly to garner the goodwill of the vendor. In Krakow, Bernhard and I had had a separate budget for bribes, but when the money was all spent, we hadn't learned anything; the Poles couldn't have been less helpful, regardless of whether we'd paid them off or not. A man with a huge lump on one cheek approached me and opened his hand to show me something that I couldn't make out. I allowed myself what little gratification I derived from producing my badge. He looked like a small animal as he slinked away. I thought about how if I had the choice, I would have stood there, taking shelter from the rain, for the rest of the day.

Number 18 was right across the street, a dilapidated dump from the turn of the last century. The rents rose, the upkeep fell. There was light coming from only a few of the windows. Up there, in one of them, she was waiting for me. I remembered once overhearing a little boy say "There must be a lot of old people living in there" as he stood peering up at a ramshackle apartment building. An elderly woman carrying three or four large plastic bags backed out of the front door. Maybe the kid was right. I held the newspaper above my head, crossed the street and made it just in time to get a hand on the door before it clicked shut. I gestured to give the impression I'd been standing there holding it open. Her gratitude blinded her to any breach of

5

entry protocol. What was she heading out for in this downpour anyway, with only a cardigan over her shoulders? I pictured her being washed away by the rain, never to emerge again. In the building where my grandmother lived, there had been a woman concierge, I thought of her for some reason.

The entrance smelled of cod-liver oil. Two names on the mailbox: Inger and Maria. A sunflower sticker distinguished it from the rest, as though they possessed some vim and courage that the other residents did not. Three flights up, the door to the apartment had a similar sign, with the same sunflower. Was this their emblem, a signal to the rest of the world to say, look at the two of us, we can roll with the punches. There were sounds from the neighboring apartment, at first I thought they were coming from hers. A man yelled, then a fainter voice, that of a woman or child, replied, although it was impossible to make out what either of them were saying. There was a crash. Something broke. Then it went quiet.

I tried to imagine her, form a picture of who she was, the woman I would meet in just a moment. How did she spend these interminable days alone? What went through her mind when she woke up each morning and realized once again that her daughter was gone?

I didn't want to go in. I didn't want to meet her. I didn't want to have anything to do with her, nor the damned case. I'd been the first officer on the scene of a murder once. A young girl had been found lying under the tarpaulin of a rowboat in an old boathouse. The tip of a bottleneck had been sticking out from between her legs, and a scarf had been jammed into her mouth with such force that her tongue had almost been torn out.

The face that appeared in the crack in the door caught me off guard. It was so beautiful. How could a woman who had lost her child be beautiful?

"I thought you'd forgotten," she said, after I had introduced myself. Then she opened the door all the way. Her face had a gray pallor, only noticeable to me upon entering. In the hallway, exposed under the light of her own home, it was as though her grief were developed photographically and held up in front of me, like something I was obliged to examine. But the sorrow was in no way recent. It was a gray mask of hardened, crumbling despair. I removed my shoes. I stood holding them in my hands, listening to the drips hit the floor, then noticed that my socks were also wet and visualized the glistening footprints I would leave behind when I began to walk, the naked impressions on an unfamiliar floor. She smiled. I probably looked ridiculous standing there. I felt like a grown-up in a doll's house. She took my shoes from me and asked me to come on in.

As I walked along the soft carpet in the hall, I realized how hopeless the whole situation was. I should never have agreed to meet her. I'd only spoken to her once over the phone. She'd called the day the case had been officially passed on to me. I'd only just begun going through the list of documents when the phone rang. Perhaps she had a sixth sense for anything related to her daughter's case? She'd started asking questions almost immediately: what I was planning to do, what I was bringing to the investigation, what measures I had in mind to find new leads, and, eventually, how long I figured it would take before I found her. What was I supposed to tell her? The whole point of passing the case on to me was to set it aside. Officially, I was prohibited from undertaking any action unless a new line of inquiry turned up that forced me to. The investigation was to be considered ongoing and this was to be achieved by my doing nothing. I was ordered to keep watch over a corpse.

But that wasn't good enough for her; she wanted to know when I would come to see her, wanted to set a time there and then.

As soon as we entered the living room she started asking questions. And instead of the broken-down desperation that I realized I had, to a certain degree, prepared myself to have to deal with, I was met with an alert, quick-witted person who confronted me directly with the facts of the case in an onslaught of pent-up despair, with almost aggressive frustration. She posed questions. She demanded answers. I gathered it had been a while since she'd had any contact with the investigators, and that that was why she'd acted so quickly when I'd come into the picture. She probably presumed that with a new man on the case, everything would start over again, all avenues would be open to exploration and the chances of finding her daughter would be as good as they were twelve months ago. And as hope was rekindled, so sorrow was roused. This fresh hope allowed despair to gain admittance. Everything that had lain dormant, that had begun to resemble a state of normality, was abruptly awoken again, and was going to be relived anew.

The answers I was able to give her were in all likelihood as vague and indeterminate as she had feared. It was hell for her to listen to my hollow assurances. Of course we're doing what we can. Yes, we're keeping all lines of inquiry open. As soon as something turns up, all our resources will be brought to bear.

It was an act. There was something rehearsed about it, the entire conversation, her despairing demands as much as my pathetic evasions and equivocations. Yes, even she and everything she said bore the loathsome air of a *sham*, of lines learned by heart, of tirades, of just being reeled off: she had said all this before, a hundred times and more, had badgered my colleagues with it every opportunity she got, every single time any of them had come within range of her. That was the reason for the horrible things they said about her down at the station. Bad jokes abounded. Malicious jokes. She had become a caricature.

But it had gone on too long, with little to show, and none of the investigators who worked the case managed to sustain the compassion they'd had at the outset. Instead of the mother they all wanted to help, she became the tormentor they could not shake. The dissatisfaction among the police involved frustration over developments which failed to come about, and her own deepening powerlessness with regard to the nightmare which played out had driven the two parties apart. The energy that should have impelled them towards their common goal had turned them against one another. She criticized them and they admonished her. Hope dwindled. None of them could face her anymore. They had stood behind me making victory signs the day the documents list was handed over to me. The entire thing was a mess. And it landed with a smack on my desk.

"It's just you, isn't it?" she said.

I understood what she meant but pretended not to.

"There's nobody else working on it anymore. It's just you."

"At this point in time I'm the sole investigator. But as soon . . ."

"As soon as any fresh information comes to light," she said, mimicking me.

I acted like I had not heard her.

"Yes," I said, "the moment . . ."

"But no fresh leads have turned up. They've said that the whole time, but no fresh leads ever turn up. No fresh leads are going to turn up if you don't do something to make it happen."

"It's been a year. It's just not possible to maintain the momentum that was there to begin with."

"And meanwhile she's out there somewhere this whole time while nothing happens. She's there all the time. She's there all the time. Maria is someplace or another at this very moment while the two of us sit here talking. Do you understand that?"

I knew that no matter what I said it would only fan the flames. It was eating away at her from inside. I was merely the latest addition, there to put her through all the pain once again.

"It doesn't mean the case has been closed," I said. "A case like this is never shelved. But it is quite impossible for us to dedicate our full resources to something over . . ."

I hesitated.

"Over such a long time . . . ?" she said.

Her irony was cruel.

"You've given up, haven't you?" she continued. "The lot of you, that's what you've done? This here, the fact that you came to see me, it's just a formality, just bullshit, it doesn't mean a thing. You all gave up a long time ago. It's been ages since you all realized you weren't going to get anywhere."

"People have been found after longer periods than this . . ."

"And then you come here, trying to pretend as though you're still hard at it, still believe that you'll manage to find her."

She stood up, began moving around.

"How dare you!" She gesticulated wildly. "How dare you show up here, when you know that! When you know that's how it is! When you know that there is no more, that nothing else is going to happen!"

Practically every rule had been broken in the space of the half-hour I'd spent there. At the same time, or perhaps precisely because of that, I had also passed the point where I could take my leave. I had begun listening to her and had to hear her out. She needed me for a little while yet. I had to stay until she was finished, until she allowed me to leave. Then it would be over, and there wouldn't be anything more I could do for her. When nothing else had led anywhere, the least I could do was see this through.

"What if she's tied up someplace, what if she's locked in, being abused by some maniac? What if someone is forcing himself on her right now? Right this minute? What if some bastard is at her right now?"

She let out a howl, her face contorted. She stood roaring, as a deep, disturbing voice, sounding more like that of an animal than her own, was drawn out of her. I got to my feet but was at a loss as to what to do. I could have reached her if I stretched out my arm, but I didn't dare, I thought she might fall apart if I touched her.

She calmed down.

Then she turned away, ashamed.

"Is there anyone . . . ," I said, "who could come over . . . if you want me to ring somebody . . ."

"I'm sorry," she said. "I'm sorry."

We sat down.

I looked at her, she stared right past me. Her face was constantly changing, never settling down, never resting in the same expression long enough for it to take shape, unify into its constituent features and arrive at a countenance. What was it that I had found so beautiful? It looked like gray tissue had been pulled over red tissue. With another gray membrane beneath that again. Which in turn had been pulled over a skin-colored layer. Layer upon layer. Somewhere within all this was the life she had lived, the individual she had been, right up until the 27th of April last year. It was a person who was never coming back.

I had been sitting with her file for most of the day. There was a whole life there, within the binder. Everything. Childhood friends. Teenage romances. A lover she'd had while married. Her parents' backgrounds and their parents' backgrounds. Maria's father. The father's parents. Their parents again. Pages of printouts. As though my colleagues, in the absence of suspects, had expended their energy digging up whatever they could on her and the husband, brought them in every time they had nobody else to question. In their uncertainty over where to focus attention they had focused it on them. Everything else exhausted, finished, and rounded off. All conceivable angles checked out, all possible suspects crossed out. The entire thing had been turned inside out long before it fell into my hands. I looked at her and considered how there wasn't a single question I could ask that hadn't been put to her before. There was nothing I could do. There was no point in me being there.

There was a shelf lined with books behind where she sat.

Most of the spines were worn, the paperbacks had long, white cracks running down them, rendering most of the titles illegible. A CD player and a cordless telephone sat on the foldout of an old escritoire. The contrast between old and new in the decor gave the impression of carefully considered choices, of taste. Choices that were now divested of all value, as the whole time everything had been moving towards this. When she bought this apartment and began to furnish it, I thought, converting it into a home that would suit her and her daughter's needs, it was this that awaited them, this unimaginable suffering they had already been heading towards. When she divorced her husband, took her daughter, and moved in here, she was also already on her way towards this. When she finally made up her mind that it was the right thing to do, this was the direction everything was moving in. When they slept here, Maria and she, that first night with moving boxes all around them . . . When she agreed to Maria getting her own mobile phone, keeping in mind the trips back and forth between her apartment and her father's . . . When she signed the divorce papers with her husband . . . When she screamed at him in anger when all three of them sat at the table to eat, even then they had been heading towards this. All the times she praised her daughter, all the times she scolded her, the times she sang for her, when she bought clothes for her, when she convinced her to begin karate lessons, when she argued with her because she abruptly and without any apparent reason wanted to quit . . . Everything had been leading up to this.

This had been the purpose of all things, that night in April when she had sent her daughter with the money to go to the shop, two blocks over, just before closing time, having just showered and not wanting to go out with wet hair, and having asked Maria if she could be so kind as to do it, telling her to take a hundred kroner from the handbag hanging in the hallway, calling out after her, as she heard the front door being opened, to remember to wear a hat, and then going back into the bathroom to dry her hair.

My telephone vibrated with the sound of an incoming text, playing a short, all too cheerful melody.

I apologized as I reached to check it, although I already knew who it was before I had opened the message. ANNE-SOFIE: *You back soon?*

I turned off the mobile and put it back in my jacket.

"Wait," she said. "Please. Don't leave."

She looked at the table as though someone had just placed it there.

"Would you like something? Coffee?"

"No, thank you. I need to be getting off soon."

She nodded—in the direction of the pocket where I had placed the mobile, if I interpreted her correctly. She took a deep breath before she said it.

"Kids?"

"No," I replied, uneasy at the familiarity I'd gotten tangled in, that she had entangled me in. Why had the conversation turned into one I had no control over? How on earth was it any of this person's business who it was that had sent me a text? How had things arrived at the stage where the possibility of not answering didn't cross my mind?

"It was my wife."

She smiled, a somber, heart-rending smile. Now I recognized the face I had seen in the doorway.

And I had a sudden impulse to tell her about Anne-Sofie, felt I had an opportunity, a possibility, an opening that would never return.

But the feeling only lasted a moment. Then the whole situation seemed even more uncomfortable to me. The two of us sitting across from one another, on our own, the living room window like the glass of an aquarium, as though nothing other than this existed and no one apart from us were alive. All at once it felt absolutely unbearable to be sitting there with her, broaching personal matters, listening to her confessions, responding with consolation, with consideration, with the most calculated form of compassion, simply because I couldn't desist.

I regretted having turned off the phone, I thought about how a new message from Anne-Sofie, which I was pretty sure had already been sent and lay waiting, was just what I needed to extricate myself, find my shoes, get out of there and never come back.

I noticed she was looking at me. Eventually I had to look up. Our eyes met. She held my gaze.

"It'll be a year tomorrow," she said. "When do you think you'll find her?"

I waited as long as I could, as I had done outside on the street, before making a move to leave. I let her speak and felt I regained some of my professional distance, which at one point she had managed to deprive me of completely. I didn't need to say anything, she wasn't out after answers anymore, but just wanted to talk, to keep fear at bay, be somewhere else, with someone else. Her voice kept her together, prevented her from falling apart. The fact that someone listened to it, that it was still possible to understand what it articulated, held promise. But at the same time, a faint but shrill note cut constantly through it, her tone of voice was beyond her control.

Time passed. I thought about Anne-Sofie. But I had to wait until Inger Danielsen was finished talking. When she was alone again her voice would not provide any succor, then it too would become part of everything frightening and dreadful. Did she talk to herself? All those hours spent alone with that unbearable weight, poring over the same things again and again, all the possibilities, all the fears, and all the outcomes imaginable.

In the hallway, I found a crumpled-up newspaper page in each shoe, without being able to understand when she'd availed of the opportunity to put them in, she had after all been in the same room as me from the time I arrived until I left? As I was making my way down the stairs, a door opened somewhere below, and when I looked over the banister I saw the elderly lady, all wrapped up against the elements this time, hurrying past the rows of mailboxes, which down in the perpetual dusk of the entrance resembled two enormous rows of teeth.

She stopped suddenly and looked up, caught sight of me and called out: "Are you a resident?"

My first thought was to pull back, pretend I hadn't heard, my next was to lie and put the cheeky old biddy in her place, but finally I realized that I had no reason to do either of the two.

"No," I replied, startled by how my own voice resounded within the shaft of the stairwell. "Just visiting!"

Then she smiled, as though any other answer would have ruined her day. Seemingly satisfied, she gathered her raincoat tighter around her and walked towards the exit, to be engulfed by the rain once more.

I'd been dying to get outside, but it was like moving from one cramped space to another. People were standing huddled wherever an overhanging roof or awning was to be found. Steam rose from the newsstand on the other side of the road, making it appear as though a fire had just been put out.

I peered up at the front of the apartment block, squinting in the rain, located the window I thought was hers but wanted to see her face, or a shadow on the curtains to confirm it. Why wasn't it visible, why wasn't it possible to see that a girl from this building had gone missing? Why did the apartment block, stairwell, name on the door, all look the same, after the terrible thing that had occurred here? Her mother had forgotten to buy milk, according to the case file, she had remembered to buy Honey Smacks, which was the only thing the girl would eat at the time, but had forgotten to buy milk: it was the daughter who had realized it when she was going to make supper, ten minutes before the corner shop closed.

I walked to the subway station, switching on my phone as I ran down the steps, a new message came in after just a few seconds, I didn't need to check who it was from. Then one more. Then another. Then one after that. There was a smell in the train compartment like that of a stable, from the streaming, sweaty bodies side by side in wet clothes. The windows were misted: beads of water began moving as soon as the train was underway. I found an unoccupied seat but the fug was unbearable, I breathed through my mouth and checked the last text from Anne-Sofie, which consisted solely of two question marks.

I looked at the window, the drops of water had extended to resemble twigs. There was something unreal about the racket and shaking of the coaches as the train made it to top speed. It was like a fit of rage. Advertisements slammed past inside the tunnel, it seemed like they hit the window before being hurled back. We sat in the midst of the tumult, of the fury, of the subterranean rumble. I glanced up at the passengers closest to me. But they just stood there, tired, impatient, half-asleep, as though nothing could happen to alter that state.

The most natural thing, considering how late I was, would be for her to call out when she heard me come in the door. Instead I was the one who announced myself. I heard her reply, but not what she said, nor which room it came from. As usual, I hoped it had come from the living room, that she was up and dressed.

She was sitting on the sofa with a blanket over her and the lights off. The TV was on, glowing blue, but the volume was so low that she couldn't possibly hear anything that was being said. I went over and kissed her on the top of the head.

"Where have you been?" She spoke in a low tone, hardly moving her lips, her own sound level adjusted to that of the TV.

"I had to take care of something after I left the station."

"Where?"

"How are you feeling?"

"It's back again, same as before. It gets worse as the day goes on."

She groaned, mumbled something.

"What did you say?" I spoke a little louder, thinking perhaps it might prompt her into doing the same.

"I think I'm going crazy," she said.

I looked around the room. The curtains were drawn. The vase and candelabra that usually stood on the dining table were both on the floor, and something large and dark was in their place.

"Would you not like a little more light?"

I leaned over her and switched on one of the wall lamps above the sofa. She held her hand up in front of her eyes.

"Please."

The short burst of light made the darkness even deeper in its absence, the room suddenly seemed enormous, infinite, for a moment I got it into my head we were standing outdoors.

"Why were you so late?"

"It's that new case. I had to call on someone."

"Who?"

"A mother. The mother of the little girl who's missing."

"At her place?"

"What do you mean?"

"Were you at her place?"

"Yeah."

"Is she pretty?"

"Pretty? Jesus. I hadn't even thought about it."

"Hadn't thought about it? Why do you say that and not just whether she is or she isn't?"

"Because I haven't thought about it. Because that's not what you think about when you meet a person whose child is missing."

She went quiet.

"Have you eaten?"

She didn't reply.

"Will I make you a bite to eat?"

She mumbled something.

"What did you say?"

"I don't think I can face food. But you have something."

I went into the kitchen. The fridge door was ajar, a bottle of mineral water not quite allowing it to close, something lying on the top shelf had been left open and dripped sticky lumps on to the shelves below. Some cheese that hadn't been wrapped back up again properly lay on the kitchen bench. I took out a pepperoni sausage, a tube of mayonnaise, some tomatoes and butter, cut away the hard edge of the cheese, found a few slices of bread and placed everything on a tray together with two plates and some cutlery, put some coffee on and tapped half a glass from the box of red wine. The steam from the coffee maker resembled that immense cloud outside that never ran dry.

I carried the tray into the living room, cleared some space for it on the glass table in front of the sofa and sat down beside her. There was a discussion program on the TV, I recognized some of the participants but couldn't make out what any of them were saying. I tried to get her to eat but she refused. I turned up the volume, went into the kitchen, refilled my glass, and when I returned I had the feeling she'd turned the sound back down, but I couldn't be sure.

"What's that?" I nodded in the direction of the dining table.

"My karakul coat."

"What's it doing there?"

"I was trying to repair it."

"Surely you don't need it at the moment?"

"A seam's come apart."

I loosened my tie and undid the top button of my shirt, it had to be way over twenty degrees in the room, stifling.

"Aren't you warm?" I asked. She was sitting with the blanket pulled up under her chin. I gave it a tug but she just tightened her grip. I switched the channel, the news would be starting soon. She made no comment. After a while she got to her feet, her mobile phone fell to the floor as she rose.

"Are you coming?" she asked. I saw now that she was wearing a nightdress.

"I'll be in soon."

"Are you going to visit her again tomorrow?"

"Who?"

"You know who I mean."

"I'm not sure. I've only just been handed the case."

"Which means you are," she said. "If you could manage to be honest with me, Kristian, instead of persisting with all these lies of yours."

I turned on both wall lamps when she left, the light dazzling my eyes. I picked up her mobile, pressed on sent messages, saw my own name, scrolled down, the column appeared never-ending, my name running on and on, reproducing itself an infinite number of times.

Kristian
Kristian
Kristian
Kristian
Kristian
Kristian
Kristian
Kristian
Kristian

I reached for the remote control and flicked through the TV stations, a movie had just begun on one of them. The opening credits were stylish, the text gliding over the bonnet and windshield of a car driving slowly down a street, looking like glowing neon signs. I continued watching, without following the plot, merely enjoying the stylized inaccuracies, all the errors and unlikely aspects in the representation of police work. I tried to think of how many policemen in total had been depicted on film, pictured them gathered in a troupe, a crowd of people, a swaying wheat field, some in uniform, others in plain clothes, and I thought about the dream nearly every small boy has had, as if all the movies that had ever been made about policemen, and ever would be made, were a fulfillment of that fantasy all men had once shared.

A brief article appeared in the newspaper the next day, just one column, along with a small photograph, the same one as had been used in previous news reports. It was from the girl's own album, not chosen on account of it being the best, but because it was the last one taken of her. It was from a café in a bowling alley, and I knew that in the original picture she had a friend on either side and was standing holding a soda cup, but now only her head and part of her shoulders were visible and it had been so enlarged that she was unrecognizable. Her pupils were glowing red. Why hadn't they taken the trouble to fix that? Who on earth could claim to identify this red-eyed monster in a crowd on a street? No one would know her at all. Or she was someone everybody knew. Tips had flooded in the first few weeks, calls from all over the country, even a few from abroad, she'd been seen in cinema foyers, bus stations, train stations, airports, cafés, in cars and coaches, on the street at all hours, in red-light districts, parks where drugs were being sold, she was spotted alone and together with others, a retired fireman had called from Greece and swore that it had been her he'd seen on the beach that morning wearing a blue bikini, in the company of a German couple who didn't seem to want to let her out of their sight.

NO TRACE: One year since disappearance of Maria (14), it said beneath the photo. The parentheses had accompanied her name from the day the story broke. She wasn't Maria any longer, she was Maria (14). Plucked from the world of the living the day she first appeared in the newspapers.

She had been reported missing the night of the 27th of April. However, her parents wanted to keep the media away for as long

as possible. As though that would be crossing a line, and as long
as it didn't appear in the papers there was a chance she could
suddenly call and ask them to come pick her up someplace.
Eventually there was no way back. A local paper in the father's
hometown had got wind of it, no one knew how. An impromptu
press conference was arranged. Within three weeks the largest
tabloids had dubbed it the MARIA CASE. From then on cov-
erage had diminished to sporadic updates, sometimes a whole
page summing up the investigation so far, or stating the absence
of any "new developments." The storm subsided. Everything
gradually wound down, was taken apart and dismantled like
scaffolding that had served its purpose.

Everything wound down, apart from the parent's anguish
over what had happened.

From twenty men to twelve men. From twelve men to eight.
From eight to three. From three to one.

The twenty were assigned in the belief she'd be found, possibly suffering from mental or physical injury, perhaps trauma-
tized, but alive, or safe and sound for all they knew, in dubious
company but unharmed, within a few hours, a few days, that
it was only a question of time before she was returned to her
mother.

The twelve were an admission that they were abandoning
hope of her being found alive, but were still certain they'd locate
her and subsequently find the person or people responsible for
her abduction and murder.

The eight were the final belief they would find her, dumped
in a basement, on a trash heap, buried in the woods someplace,
at the bottom of a lake, that they would find her, but wouldn't
necessarily find the person or people who had put her there, or
rather that it was highly unlikely they would do so.

The three were the ones who were to wind up the case in
such a way as not to offend the family, to collect all the docu-
mentation concerning it and put it aside, so it was ready to be

retrieved when the day came, however many years in the future that might be, when the spring thaw revealed her remains in a place where searching for her had never been discussed.

The three, my predecessors, were the ones who were supposed to wrap up the case. So what on earth was left for me to do?

Risberg's justification was that they needed a fresh pair of eyes, a review of the entire investigation by someone who hadn't been on the case. To what purpose? To file it away with a cleaner conscience. In reality, the case had been lying dormant for the past six months. What I'd been assigned to do was summarize, conclude, and round off, conduct one final analysis, before the whole thing was put away. History would say that the police had done everything within their power to solve the *Maria Case*. The lawyer had included a memorandum stating that due to the extreme lack of evidence, it would prove difficult, if not impossible, to bring charges against any of the parties mentioned unless a confession formed the basis of a prosecution.

I didn't recognize her voice straight away when I picked up the office phone. She didn't say much, just that she'd been so confused after I had departed the day before. She'd paced the apartment for several hours thinking about everything she'd wished she had said, all the things she'd actually planned to say but hadn't. She had difficulty, she said, remembering what we had talked about, was uncertain about what was said and what was not, didn't know if anything had come from the conversation, had no indication, she felt, of what was going to take place now, wondered if we could meet again, sit down and go through it all, not, she assured me, to demand more of me than I could deliver, but to have something concrete to relate to. She told me she had not slept all night, just lain awake thinking until it grew bright, and still it was impossible for her to find some sense of calm, she was seeing double, was unable to keep her thoughts in check, if I could just help her with that, help her get her thoughts straight.

When I entered the living room there was already a thermos and a plate of cookies on the table. But there was something else, something different from the last time. The room was not as cold. And there was a smell that had been absent on my previous visit. And a sound, it was coming from a raised fireplace in the center of the room: behind two glass doors blackened with soot you could just discern the flames. I thought of Anne-Sofie. Something gnawed away at me, as always when I was away from her. But she would probably be better able to handle me coming home late than me ringing to say I would be.

"I didn't offer you anything the last time you were here," she said when we sat down. I looked around. It wasn't just the room, the whole apartment had an everyday air about it that had been absent on my previous visit, as though everything had changed back to normal in the past twenty-four hours, as though she was taking pains to show it, *the home*, in another light.

This, I thought, was how it was when Maria lived here. She wants to show me the way things were. And I tried to envision it prior to the disappearance, picture the person who had lived here with her, sat with her in the kitchen eating breakfast, shared the sofa in the evenings watching TV, gone out the front door, come back in again, been spoken to warmly, been spoken to sternly, the girl with the big, doughy, enlarged face and the two glowing red dots for eyes.

"What happened," she said, "was that I was forced to go through everything. Think through all the possibilities."

She looked at me with a hopeless expression.

"Absolutely everything. Do you understand?"

I said that I did.

"I had to look at everybody I knew. Everyone who had anything at all to do with Maria. I had to try to imagine if it could have been one of them, if it was conceivable that they had . . . done something. I had to contemplate everything. Consider everyone I knew. I went through each of them in turn. Racked my brain to remember everything I could about them. Tried to think if there'd ever been any particular situations involving them and her, things said, things I hadn't picked up on at the time, but which might in retrospect reveal something significant. Something which could give them away, expose them as the ones who had taken her."

She laughed, a distant look in her eyes.

"Some days every one of them were kidnappers and murderers. You all . . ."

"Us?"

"The police. Your colleagues. They wanted me to do it the whole time, encouraged me to think of everyone who had anything to do with her, if there was something there, they never stopped, if I could think of anything which may be of importance, anything which might point in some direction. Almost as if they weren't willing to give in until I gave them the name of the man who had done it. Almost as if . . ."

She bowed her head.

"Even Halvard. I was sitting one night . . . I think eventually I must have gone through every single thing we had ever said to one another, every hour we had spent together since Maria was born. I was sitting thinking about all the times he'd been alone with her, thinking the most terrible things, trying as hard as I could to visualize the unimaginable . . . the most unimaginable . . . I pictured it . . . I saw it happen . . . over and over again . . . I have seen him do all manner of . . . I thought about when she was at his place, on the weekends. How she hardly ever told me anything when she came back home, not unless I asked her, that she never mentioned what they had done, how they'd spent the time, if they'd gone anyplace, done anything together, what they'd talked about, how she'd found it. And then I thought that the reason she doesn't, the reason why she doesn't say anything unless I ask . . . Christ. It became sick. Do you understand? Utterly sick."

When I told her yet again that I did, it was not a lie. I had
seen it before. I had been involved in it, been part of it myself,
had personally been obliged to encourage and prompt people
into doing it, coaxed mothers into viewing their husbands as
suspects, asked friends to regard one another as frauds and swin-
dlers. Nobody comes away from it unscathed. Everything is
tarnished. Suspicion is the only thing that survives.

"Jesus, I'm talking as if I don't have . . . I'm sorry. I've done
too much thinking."

She laughed at herself.

"That's what I do. That's the only thing I've done these past
months. Thought and thought. Thought about why things are
how they are, why things turned out the way they did between
Halvard and me. Why things end up like that. And then I think
about how things were the first few days he was here again, after
Maria disappeared. It was just like . . . He was so like himself,
the way he used to be . . . And then I thought that maybe that's
what he did back then too, that he pulled himself together, that
all the care and attention he showed me, that it was an effort on
his part, that this was something he does when he feels duty-
bound, when he feels the situation demands it of him. That it's
not something that comes naturally to him. That he can be like
that if he wants. But it's not something that he just has within
him. That his silence, his reticence and aloofness, they denote
the real him. All his other qualities are just a supplement of sorts.
Something he marshals when he must. What do you think?"

But she didn't look like she was expecting any answer.

"Are you yourself again?" she said. "I remember my mother
asking me that after I'd split up with a boy in high school and
had been moping around brokenhearted for a few weeks."

It could have been a normal conversation between two
friends. Between two people not damaged from before. As
though we had been brought together under the most normal of
circumstances, a chance meeting, or through friends of friends.

"But I knew, I think, right from the start, as soon as we got together, that we'd split up in the end, that it wouldn't last. Part of me remained calmly on the outside of everything, and that part of me saw a man who I'd never be genuinely close to. But all the ways we encouraged each other . . . the resourcefulness we suddenly had . . . the courage."

She had a faraway look in her eyes that I liked.

"Two people who begin by bringing out the best in one another," she said, "and end up bringing out the worst."

It could have been a completely ordinary conversation. Until she suddenly caught her breath and her features dissolved in front of me. For a few moments she was unrecognizable.

"Christ!" she said, holding her hands in front of her face.

Then she calmed down, took up where she left off and continued to speak. But there was something strained about her voice, even when she wasn't talking about the case, a fragility was present, a stifled hysteria that could break through at any moment.

She forgot what had happened and she remembered it again. It came and went all the time, it wasn't possible for it to maintain a sustained presence, it would have broken her down completely if it had. She forgot what had happened then remembered it again. She wavered between forgetfulness and terrible awakening. It was like a force outside her, it crashed like a wave, then receded. Washed over her. And then it was gone. Washed over her again. And was gone once more.

"When I saw Halvard, when he came here, the morning after that night . . ."

She pressed her eyes shut, pinched her fingers hard against the root of her nose, a long teardrop squeezed out from one eye. "I just stood there staring at him . . . as though it would somehow be possible to see it. That if it was him then it would show. And he stood there unable to understand a thing. He asked what it was. And I just stared and stared and waited for him to break down and confess. I figured if I stood there long enough looking at him it would come, he wouldn't be able to hold back any

longer. Poor man. He stayed here for a while. There was no end
to the things he could do for me. It was like it had been earlier.
It was almost like it had been at the very start! So attentive and
considerate, just like when we first met. All the small things. I
asked him what Kristina thought about him sleeping over at
my place. He said that this took precedence over everything,
that he wouldn't hear of anything else. Neither would Kristina.
She even called me one day, wondered if there was anything
she could help me with. The last time we'd met before that we
hadn't exchanged a word. Ignored each other completely. She'd
accompanied him when he'd popped in to drop off something
Maria had forgotten."

She looked at me as though waiting for me to give the cue,
which she would then respect, of my not wanting to hear any
more.

"He stayed here for a week. It was grotesque. It was like back
when we first met and fell in love. As though we had started
over. I recalled things I'd forgotten from when we were first
together. He did too. He began to tell me about things, things
he remembered, which he had cherished, which he had never
spoken of before. We sat there night after night, talking about
trips we'd taken, things we'd done. That first summer together,
he told me, he had been woken up once by his own laughter,
he was lying in bed laughing out loud, unable to stop. But then
one night . . ."

What was she about to tell me? What was it I was letting
myself in for?

But it was too late to cut her short, to ask her to stop.

"We were in my room . . . ," she continued. "He couldn't face
sleeping in Maria's bedroom . . . And then . . . that night . . . he
wanted to make love . . ."

I knew what I needed to do, everything within me told me
that I had to do it, and do it now: interrupt her, get to my feet,
leave and shut the door behind me. But I did not. I gave her no

cue. I remained sitting listening, as though there was nothing I would rather do.

"I couldn't fathom it, how he could have any desire, how he could feel like doing anything like that. After he left, I threw up. Stuffed the bedclothes into the washing machine and began cleaning the entire room, the floor, the walls, the ceiling, everything, all through the night, until it grew bright."

I pictured it, him all worked up, her quite still, offering no resistance.

"But he finds it easier to compartmentalize. Separate one thing from another. He did it even then. Like the days when he was staying here, he'd be humming all of a sudden or cracking up at something on the TV. He could suggest, in a cheerful way, quite out of the blue, that we go out for a stroll, as though nothing had happened. I didn't understand it. I couldn't understand it if I wanted to, even if I tried. But that's the way he is. He needs to compartmentalize. He has a video game at home, one where you race cars. He told me once that Kristina gets on at him, that she can't stand it, him sitting there completely absorbed in it."

Why would I want to know that? I wondered if she expected something of me. But it seemed like it was enough for me to sit and listen.

"I think that might be the reason. I've thought about it now. I hadn't before. But I believe that was it, that was part of the reason we split up, that the stages were so different, and became more and more at odds. His phases and my phases. The transition from one to the other. As if they never came after one another, were never in step. That there was a discrepancy the whole time. We were never in the same place simultaneously. When one of us got there the other had left."

A moment of silence arose.

I nodded to show I was listening.

"And then I think about how it was at the start, when everything was so good between us. And it's like I don't quite understand what it was that made it so good. If there was something there that was later lost, some accord, a harmony or tempo."

She smiled, a look of slight puzzlement on her face.

"That's what love does, it lifts us, carries us dry-shod over a strong current, where we'd be swept away from each other if we tried to make it across on our own."

She looked at me.

"But all this must sound completely abject?"

A police car came down the street at a snail's pace. I waved it down, my badge in my hand. It signaled and pulled up at the curb like a taxi. I got in. I recognized both of the patrolmen but didn't know their names. The driver was a woman, she asked me where I was going, I thought about Anne-Sofie but replied that I didn't know, that they could take me on their rounds, anything as long as it meant I avoided walking in that deluge out there.

We glided through the streets. I told them about my car and said that an inspector without a car was like a crow without wings. Neither of them laughed.

The raindrops on the window glowed yellow. The radio crackled now and again, rasping voices exchanging words. The patrolman said something to his female counterpart I wasn't able to catch. I got the feeling they didn't like each other and they were annoyed at having been sent out together, I wondered if it could have something to do with the fact she was the one driving and not him.

"Quiet night?" I asked.

Neither of them replied. I leaned forward between the front seats. Just then a message came over the radio. The man reached for the microphone and said something, I didn't hear what, but I understood he had answered affirmatively to a call. He said something to his colleague, who put the lights on and sounded the siren for a few seconds until the lane ahead was clear.

"What's happening?" I yelled.

"Trouble at The Majestic," he replied. "The hookers use it. We go round there every other day."

We soon pulled up in front of a run-down building. *JES* was the only part of the name still illuminated.

"I'll come in with you," I said, feeling a peculiar tingling in my body, a sort of childish excitement, an urge to act, a rush of unused energy.

The receptionist was an elderly man with long hair.

"214," he said, and nodded towards the stairs.

"Out of order," he added, as the female officer approached the elevator.

All the 200s were on the third floor. The door to 214 was open. I thought about the ridiculous numbering, the size of the establishment taken into consideration. Hoarse screams could be heard from inside, coming at regular intervals. The male officer slipped his truncheon from his belt and entered first.

There were four people in the room, three whores and one customer. He was the one making the noise. He was wearing underwear and socks, nothing else, and was sitting on a low stool with his eyes closed, rocking back and forth. His screaming matched the rhythm of his movements. He had a towel wrapped around a hand that one of the whores was standing holding in both of hers. The bed was covered in blood.

The two other girls were by the window. One of them was dressed only in her underwear and a pair of black tights with runs in them.

"What happened here?" the female officer asked.

The one holding the makeshift bandage in place, who also appeared to be the eldest, looked towards the corner of the room. I followed the direction of her gaze and caught sight of a Sami knife on the floor behind the door.

All of a sudden the man with the injured hand seemed to come to life.

"She tried to chop my hand off!" he wheezed. "That fucking bitch tried to chop my hand off!"

"It's not too bad," the oldest whore said. "But it's pretty deep. He shouldn't wait too long before getting it seen to."

"Who did it?" I asked.

The customer turned to the girl in the underwear. "That one! That bitch there!"

"Drive him to the emergency room," I said to the two officers. "I'll take care of everything here."

The patrolman took hold of the injured party beneath the arm and helped him up.

"I'll need to get some fucking clothes on first!" he screamed. Blood had begun to seep through the towel, he held around it as though he was afraid his hand would fall off.

"I should've ruptured your fucking intestines!"

The two officers helped him put on his clothes.

"Careful!" he sobbed. "Careful!"

He sounded like a child. The rhythmic grunts still escaped him, the tempo unchanged as they led him between them down the stairs.

"I've got customers waiting," the oldest one said after they had left.

I nodded.

"Me too," the other girl said. She had been standing with her arms around her colleague in a protective fashion, but she let go now that the danger was past. It was strange: the solidarity between the whores, which had seemed so strong when we arrived, now dissipated. They left her on her own, the one responsible, she couldn't expect support from either of them.

When we were alone she draped a dressing gown over her shoulders. Then she took a packet of cigarettes from a drawer. I gave her a light and took one when it was offered.

"Are you injured?" I asked, after we had smoked for a while and she seemed a little less on edge.

She shook her head. Her eyes had a tetchy look about them, but something told me they always did, rage never far away.

I tore off a length of paper towel from a roll that was there and picked the knife up off the floor.

"You always have one of these handy?" I asked, holding it up in front of her, blood on the blade and handle.

"That prick wouldn't pay," she said, expelling the smoke with a harsh puff.

She couldn't have been more than twenty, and something fresh behind her harried bearing indicated she hadn't been in the business long. She had a confidence and boldness about her, a certain arrogance that wouldn't be subdued, couldn't be messed around with too much before it exploded. Her dressing gown had slid slightly off her shoulder, exposing it and a breast, bulging slightly above the tight-fitting bra.

She walked over to the bed and put the cigarette out in an ashtray on the nightstand. Then she tugged the sheet loose, wrapped the bloodied duvet in it and rolled the whole thing into a sausage shape at the footboard. She pulled her dressing gown tighter around her and sat down.

Voices could be heard from outside, someone on their way up the stairs, a man singing and a woman laughing. I walked over and closed the door, then stubbed out the cigarette and sat down beside her on the bed. "Don't make an issue out of it," she said. "That guy is an asshole. He roughed up a girl a couple of years back."

She shivered. I put my arm around her.

I suddenly felt her hand on my crotch.

"Please," she said. "I can't deal with any more problems right now."

Before I had a chance to compose myself she had taken hold of my dick through my trouser material. It swelled up.

"That was fast," she whispered.

I didn't know what to do. I decided not to do anything. She

unzipped my fly and eased her hand in. The next moment my cock was out. She masturbated it slowly. I looked at her. She smiled brazenly.

"Nice?" she asked.

Then she opened her mouth, without taking her eyes from mine. We sat like that for a moment. Then I placed my hand on the nape of her neck and pressed her head down.

Anne-Sofie was asleep when I arrived home. Food had been left out in the kitchen, milk, cheese, some cold cuts, the edges reddened and hard as plastic alongside a tub of butter with the lid off. I put everything away, swept the crumbs off the counter, threw out the empty packaging and dried up some spillage on the floor in front of the fridge. From the living room I heard the sound of cheerful voices, interrupted by music. I pictured Inger's apartment, the warm front room, the yellow lighting, the rain outside and the shelves containing all the books and CDs. I tried to remember how she looked, I could see her on the sofa in front of me, could clearly see her clothes and hair, but not her face, it slipped away every time I tried to call it to mind.

I thought about her and Halvard, about how they had fallen in love. Then drifted apart. How fear had steered them together anew.

I went into the living room, switched off the TV, found a bottle, and poured myself a glass. My eye was drawn, as it always is when I stand in front of the cocktail cabinet, to a crack in the wall, just beneath where a picture hangs. It was like a tiny entrance into somewhere quite different, a miniature reality. I saw a movie once where a woman had found a tooth hidden inside a hole in the wall of the apartment she'd just moved into. Or was it a man, I couldn't remember. He, or she, stood in front of a mirror, utterly perplexed, holding the tooth in their hand, while all kinds of awful thoughts raced through their mind about what on earth could have impelled the person who placed it there to do such a thing.

I needed a smoke but decided to resist, I got it into my head there was a duct going from the crack in the wall directly into the bedroom where Anne-Sofie lay. I pictured the girl in the hotel room, felt the beginnings of an erection when I recalled what she had done. I poured myself another drink. The alcohol further fuelled my imagination, I considered returning to the hotel, I figured that as long as she was scared of being charged I could get her to do anything. I stood for a while fantasizing about what this anything might be.

The Maria Case filled an entire room. It would take days to read through it all. An index covering tips that had come in, interviews of family, friends, classmates, teachers, coaches, neighbors, and people she'd had contact with on the Net. Everything from the hard disks on her mother's and father's computers was copied and printed out, notes, drawings, music files, internet logs, chat rooms she'd visited, all the webpages from her favorites folder, the address books from her email account, several hundred mails in her inbox, approximately the same amount of sent emails, along with others which were deleted but which the Tech Unit had managed to reconstruct. A printout of a diary that had been typed up word-for-word, its contents mundane, the last entry had been made three days prior to her disappearance. A copy of all the data on her mobile phone, which had been found in a trash can next to the newsstand across the street. An aerial photo of the area around the mother's apartment, three or four blocks in each direction, with the trash can and the shop marked by numbers. It looked completely idiotic: it should have been covered with digits, arrows, boxes, and dotted lines but there were only two marks, one of the place she was actually headed, the other of the spot the telephone was found. Apart from that, nothing. No trace evidence, nothing on any CCTV cameras, and no reliable sightings. She had evaporated. Vanished into thin air.

Border crossings, Interpol, known pedophiles, prostitution, child trafficking, organ smuggling, adoption agencies, everything had been done by the book. Two leads had been cleared up in the opening days of the investigation. The first was a text on her mobile from a boy six years older than her whom they also discovered had been active in one of the chat rooms. It had been sent the day she disappeared, they couldn't find any reply from Maria but the cryptic content of the text, composed partly in English and partly in Norwegian, could be construed as a reference to a secret meeting or an undisclosed location. The local police in the town where he lived brought him in for an interview and accepted the account he offered as adequate to eliminate him from further inquiries: the coded references, he explained, related to a role-playing game on the internet, *Demons Arise*, which they both played. She was Rosa and he was Greiznak, he told them, and the object of the game was to make your way to the innermost room of an enormous maze, where a diamond, Haalgaard's Eye, awaited as reward for the first to make it. The other tip was a from a garbage man who had come forward the day after her photo and description had appeared in the papers: on his way home from the waste depot on the night Maria went missing he had seen a car parked on a forest road behind the dump, the light had been on in the compartment and he had seen a girl who he believed matched the description and who looked like she was having an argument with a young man in the driver's seat. A search had been mounted for the car, a green Volvo, without success. It wasn't until two weeks later that the insurance companies helped turn up a lead: a green Volvo had been reported damaged in a fire, according to the company's files it had been sent to the scrapyard and fourteen thousand kroner in compensation had been paid out to the owner. The boy was brought in, he'd been so nervous he'd confessed to insurance fraud right away, before they even had a chance to ask him anything about Maria. The girl in the car was his girlfriend, or had been until that night, when she broke up with him: he had gotten drunk, totaled the car, set it on fire, and claimed the insurance money a few days later. The girl, who was afraid to say anything initially for fear of being arrested for complicity to fraud, confirmed his story. Later, according to the case files, the theory of Maria having run away on her own was revived, since the mother, Inger Danielsen, thought she had found the hundred-kroner note that she'd asked Maria to take to go to the shop. It had been right at the bottom of her handbag, beneath a chocolate wrapper. She had later, it said, expressed uncertainty as to whether or not it was the same note, that it had perhaps lain there all the time and Maria had taken the money as instructed.

She had vanished without a trace. It was like the ground had opened up and swallowed her. A mobile phone, discovered by a vagrant in a trash can and bearing only her fingerprints, was all that was left of her. Something had happened and it was beginning to look as though no one would ever know what. The parents weren't privy to it. The assurance they needed to find peace was taken away from them, kept out of reach. From the initial stage, where their only concern was getting Maria back home safe and sound, they had now arrived at the second, where all was uncertain, unclear, and unsettled, where they would have begged on their knees to know in detail what had befallen their daughter, no matter how terrible. From having first been afraid of the truth, they had now slipped into a condition where their days were characterized by a listless terror and the truth was all they wanted. From wanting to deny what had happened at all costs, they had come to a point where they would give everything to know.

There was, however, a comment in the father's file that stood out. It said he had been calm during the initial few interviews. So calm, in fact, that the seasoned investigator had determined it worthy of note. It was unusual to be so relaxed, most people were agitated, at least to begin with, and often had difficulty giving precise and detailed answers. While he, it was remarked, had been calm throughout, responded in a lucid manner and had ready answers to everything.

Why had the father been so composed, even though at that stage his daughter had been missing for less than twenty-four hours?

The only point, as far as it was possible to make out from the interview records, where the father had been distraught, if you could call it that, was when he was confronted with information garnered from an interview with the mother to the effect that Maria had lately expressed the desire to spend more time in one place, that the back and forth was getting a bit tiresome, and that she would rather stay at the mother's flat, since that was where she went to school and where most of her friends were. The interviewer had asked the father if he was aware of this, and if so, had he any thoughts on why this might be the case: the father then requested a break and asked for a glass of water. After he had been given the water and time to drink it, he had claimed that the opposite was the case, that on the contrary, Maria had spoken to him about staying over more at his place, and that on a number of occasions she had, according to him, gone as far as asking about switching schools, how difficult that might be, and a particular school had even been mentioned, presumably around the area he lived.

But there was not much to go on. They had hardly made any headway at all. So little that they had been compelled to blow what they did have out of proportion. If they'd had anything to go on from the start, it wouldn't have occurred to anyone to note in an interview record that the father of the missing girl had requested a glass of water.

There was a knock at the door. It was Risberg. He peered around the room, as if he had been hoping to find it empty. I had four or five files spread out on the desk in front of me, as well as a few sheets of my own notes.

"Soon as you're finished with all that we'll get it down to the archive, yeah?"

I nodded.

Something was bothering him, he stood in the doorway shifting his weight from one foot to the other.

"Probably not going to get too far with all this here," he said.

He raised his hand. "No matter, only proper, one last review before we wrap it up. But the chances of anything coming from it are limited. Very limited, I'd say."

"I was planning to go through all the interviews," I said. "If there's anything to be found, then . . ."

"It might turn up there. Yes, indeed. But . . . like I say, don't spend too much time on it. This case tied up all our resources for a while. And you can see yourself," he nodded at the shelves behind me, "how much we achieved. In my personal opinion, Wold, that girl is never going to be seen again. Never!"

He rapped on the doorframe with his knuckles a couple of times before he turned and left. It looked like he had something else on his mind, but he avoided further conversation.

Never. She did not exist anymore. She was not there, not for any of those who wanted her to be. None of the things she could enjoy, be surrounded by, take pleasure in, feel safe around could reach her any longer, because they did not know where to find her. Love and compassion existed but she did not.

My mobile rang.

"When are you coming home?"

"I don't know. I have some papers I need to look through. It's hard to say. There's quite a lot, I really would like to get as much of it out of the way as possible."

"Will you call as soon as you know when you'll be finished?"

"Yeah. How's it going?"

"The same. It never lets up. It's driving me crazy."

"Try to get some sleep."

"I think it must be these new pills, I slept better before, these new ones have the opposite effect, my head feels really strange when I wake up, like I haven't slept at all . . ."

"Still, see if you can get some sleep," I said.

"I can't take this anymore. I'm not able to. It's driving me crazy. I can't take it anymore, not one more day."

"Anne."

"I'd sooner kill myself."

"Anne. Listen. I have to sit here a while longer but as soon as I'm done," I checked my watch, "I'll call you, okay?"

It was quiet on the other end of the line but I could tell she was crying.

"Is that all right? Anne?"

She made no reply.

"I'll wrap up here and then I'll call you. Okay?"

The intercom crackled and a voice said: "Wold. There's a call for you."

"I need to take another call," I said to Anne-Sofie. "I'll ring you in a little while."

"You told me yesterday that you'd given thought to your husband . . . ," I said, not because I felt there was anything to it but because it was a place to begin, somewhere to grab hold, a thread to unwind, so it looked like something was being done.

"Halvard."

"That you'd given some thought to the possibility that it was him. You recounted how he came around the next morning and that you suspected it was him."

"That was madness. I told you that."

"I know. What I was wondering about was whether or not you'd mentioned it to any of the investigators?"

"Of course not. I explained to you how it was. It was insane. I thought the same about everyone. Why are you asking about that?"

"I just want to know if it came up at any point, if it had been assessed in any way?"

"Assessed? What do you mean?"

"Nothing. I'm merely taking into account what you related to me yesterday and looking at it with regard to what I'm reading. I was looking through the interviews with your husband today and that was why I . . ."

"But is there something about it there? Does it say something about him being a suspect?"

"No, not at all," I said. "How are things between you now, do you stay in touch?"

"He calls me up. I call him up. But there's not a great deal to say."

She shrugged.

"I could see it the last time we met, how he didn't want to talk about it, viewed it as unpleasant and wanted it over with. He can't face it anymore, can't face thinking about it. He feels we should put it behind us. Start thinking about the future. Move on. No point lingering, he's said. Maria is gone. We have to learn to live with it. Maybe someday we'll find out what happened. Maybe we'll never know. Either way, it's not to going to bring Maria back. Life goes on without her."

She paused for a moment.

"I wish I could have his attitude. I wish I could move on like him."

She looked up at me.

"That's what he tells me. If I'm planning to go on grieving over Maria then I can do it on my own. He won't be party to it. He plans to move on with his life, he has no intention of letting it come to a standstill."

"But if I were to visit him and speak to him, how do you think he'd feel about that?"

"But what do you want to talk to him about? Is there something . . . Have you come across something? Do you think he could have had something to do with this?"

"That's not the reason I ask. You need to believe me about that. But I'm talking to you now and getting a picture of the case from your point of view, so I think it's only reasonable I also get a sense of how he's experienced this past year, now that I'm going to go through all this material. You need to keep in mind that I haven't had anything to do with the case before now. This is all new to me. Whatever he has to say, whatever you have to say, it's all of interest to me."

"I don't know. He'll agree to it of course. But I don't think anything will come of it. For him, it's over with. All this is over with, as far as he's concerned. She's gone. That's it. I don't understand it. How it's possible to think that way."

"Aren't you being rather unfair?" I ventured to say. "He came across as a very caring, considerate father in his interviews. Very involved in Maria's life."

"He's been a good father. He was always there for her when she was small. It was almost a bit much at times. I remember the doctor asking me once, when I brought her along for a checkup, why it was always her father who brought her along and not me. I didn't even realize it, but she said it was the first time she'd seen me at the clinic with Maria. And when Maria wanted to show us something, something she'd made or was proud of, then he was always the one she showed it to. She might come over to me but only to ask where Daddy was. I only got to see it afterwards and that was if I asked. He had to see it first. He always had to see it first. But then, when things started getting difficult between us, it was as though he drifted away from her as well. Like he couldn't manage to live with either of us any longer. He grew more and more distant, wasn't around as much, and was less and less interested in doing things together. As though he had made up his mind that that life, with the two of us, wasn't what he wanted after all, and because that life meant an existence with the three of us together, then it was both of us, both me and Maria, that he had to leave behind."

"What about their relationship after the divorce?"

"There was a brief period where they didn't have any contact. Then he got in touch and said he'd like us to share custody, that she could live with me and have her home here, if that was what I wanted, but that he now wanted to spend as much time with her as possible."

She smiled: "I guess it was just me he wanted to get rid of."

"And how did she feel about it, dividing her time between both of you?"

"I think it meant a lot to her, that he showed her that he was still her father, that he still wanted to be part of her life even though things were over between us."

"According to the files, you mentioned that in the period just prior to her disappearance she had expressed the desire to spend more time with you and less with him?"

"Does it say that . . . ?" She seemed uncertain. "I don't remember that. Are you sure?"

"Or rather I should say it appears in the transcription of one of your husband's interviews, that you mentioned it to one of the investigating officers."

"No, I didn't say that. I couldn't have, because Maria didn't say anything like that to me either."

She looked confused.

"But what did he say about it then?"

Yet another violation of the rules, I thought. Jesus, where was I going with this?

"To begin with, he replied that he had no knowledge of it."

"And then?"

"And then that the opposite was the case, that she had intimated to him, quite recently, that she wanted to spend more time at his place."

"I don't understand that. It can't be right."

"According to your husband she had also asked if it was possible for her to change schools, to attend one closer to where he lived."

She pulled her chin in towards her throat, stared right ahead with incredulity and shook her head.

"I'm planning to speak to your husband in the near future," I said.

"He's not my husband."

"I beg your pardon, with Halvard, in the near future. And I'll raise the matter with him. Not because it's of any real importance, in all likelihood it's completely immaterial, it may even stem from inaccuracies in the interview transcription for all I know. But I would like to hear his version. So it's vital he doesn't hear about it from you before I've had a chance to speak to him, if you're all right with that?"

"I see."

It seemed as though she had tuned out, wasn't really paying attention to what I was saying.

"It's a minor detail, that's all, but if you do feel the need to bring it up I'd appreciate it if you waited until after I've spoken to him."

But she was sitting thinking of something else. I tried to follow the direction of her eyes. She was looking at the newspaper beside her on the sofa, folded up on the page with the article. After a while she picked it up and laid it on the table in front of me.

Maria (14). The parentheses resembled an implement, a huge scissors, a terrible tool with which to decapitate people.

"That gruesome picture," she said. "I can't understand why they're still using it."

She got up, went over to the fireplace and threw another log on, unhooked a framed photograph hanging on the wall beside, walked back and handed it to me. I looked at the photo. The face almost filled it entirely and was so close that most of it was out of focus, as opposed to the black material of the hood she had pulled over her head, which was so sharply in focus in one corner that the crosswise bands of tight mesh in the textile were visible, even a few golden hairs sticking out from under the woven pattern could be clearly distinguished, they resembled thin strands of silver.

"She's five years old in that," she said. "She looks more like herself there."

She began to shake.

"It's . . ." She sobbed. "It's . . . I don't know . . . It's so . . ."

Her hands trembled. "It's as though I've forgotten her," she finally managed to say. "Forgotten how she is, how she was before she disappeared . . . It's as though the last few years never existed."

She hugged herself until she brought the shaking under control.

"When I think about her now, it's like she's the one I remember," she said, pointing at the picture I was holding.

Though I just thought of it then, I nevertheless said: "I've been meaning to ask you if you had another photo. It can't be too old, but one that's better than what they've been using up till now." I handed back the picture frame. I thought about how in the wording I chose, there lay the promise of something new, something untried, something that could conceivably bring us one step further because it hadn't been put to the test before.

She immediately went to find a photo. Everything was a fresh start for her. I could have asked her to do anything at all and she would have.

She returned with an envelope filled with photographs. She handed it to me.

"Take a look through these. They're from Greece, from our holidays. See if you can find one in there."

"Wouldn't it be better if you . . . ?"

"You do it. You know best what's required."

I opened the envelope, took out the photos, quite a hefty bunch, and began to look through them. The pictures featured either her or her daughter alone, they had taken snapshots of each other. In one photo from a restaurant, as well as a couple from a beach, they were both present. In the ones taken on the beach they had their arms around each other, the girl looking down bashfully while her mother laughed to the photographer. But there was a self-consciousness about the mother as well;

something affected, it must have been somebody they did not know, no doubt a random tourist, who had taken the picture. None of the photos captured the girl's face well enough to form a clear picture of what she looked like. I realized why the investigating officers had not been able to use them: she looked away, she looked down, she held her hands in front of her face, she moved, she did not want her photo taken, moaned and groaned every time her mother produced the camera. It was like she didn't want to be there. She had no desire to go on holiday, I thought. She hadn't actually wanted to accompany her mother at all. I looked through all the photos again. The mother: smiling, teasing, enjoying, carefree, and relaxed. The daughter: eyes downcast, eyes closed, grimacing, turned away, out of focus. She didn't want to be there, she wanted to leave, didn't want her photo taken, she felt like a prisoner: anything at all, just not this.

"No boyfriend?" I asked. "You're quite sure about that?"

In one picture, I only noticed now, looking through them for the second time, the camera had actually managed to catch her looking directly in the lens. She was sitting with her knees drawn up, feet buried in the sand, glancing up, probably because the photographer, who must have been the mother this time, had just called out to her. Unfortunately her whole face was not visible, her knees were in the way, but there was something in her expression that, the more I examined it, told me that this was what she looked like, had looked like, still looked like, unless she was lying someplace, her true features twisted, stiffened into an unrecognizable grimace, a frightful deathly countenance.

I placed the picture from Greece beside the missing-person photo in the newspaper. It was like looking at two different people, two individuals who had nothing to do with each other. One of them, the girl glancing up and being herself for the merest instant before managing to pull back out of sight, I was sure I would recognize as soon as I saw her, the other could have been anybody, or no one at all, a girl it was not possible to imagine existed out there, waiting for help that would not come. It was like night and day. One living and one dead.

"I trust you won't be spending too much more time on the Maria Case before you're done with it," Risberg said, giving the air of a friendly request to what in reality was an incontestable order.

He was back again an hour later. He glanced discontentedly at the files. Then he handed me a Post-it note with the name of a hospital, a department, and a room number.

"Tove Gunerius," he said. "Wife of the hotel mogul. Was admitted a couple weeks ago. Both kneecaps cut off. Crippled. Doubtful she'll ever be able to stand unassisted. She says it was an accident, some machine or another their gardener uses. The doctor has had his doubts from the get-go and finally decided to notify us. I want you to go over there and have a chat with her."

I took the note and stuck it to the edge of the desk, running my thumb over it a couple of times to get it to adhere properly.

"Now," Risberg said.

The calmness of his voice underscored the irritation behind it. He remained standing in the doorway, wanted to make sure I tore myself away from the Maria Case and left. I took a random stack of papers with me on the way out to placate him.

"I don't know what the fuck it could be," Risberg said. "Gunerius has been involved in all kinds. It's got more than a whiff of loan sharks about it. Wouldn't surprise me if he's busy concocting some way to get back at them now. We can try and put a stop to that, if nothing else."

"You can drop by and see Gunerius as well!" he called after me as I stepped into the elevator. He was still standing in the same spot as the doors closed: I pictured my office being filled with officers a moment later, who, on Risberg's orders, began emptying it entirely of paperwork while I was on my way down through the floors.

Mrs. Gunerius was a ridiculous sight. Her legs, which were plas-
tered and elevated high in traction, were concealed beneath a
large white sheet, making it look like her body, judging by the
small head on the pillow, ended in an enormous pair of feet. She
seemed groggy, as though she'd just fallen asleep. I sat down on
a chair beside the bed, showed her my badge and asked how
she was.

She looked at me, drowsily, then turned her head away. The
nurse had given me ten minutes, it felt like I had used most of
my allotted time up already.

"You informed the doctor that your injuries were the result
of an accident," I continued. "However, we have our doubts as
to whether that's actually the case. As have the doctors who
examined you."

She lay there with her face turned away.

"Are you sure you don't have anything you want to tell me?"
I said, aware of the sound of my own voice in the room, how
uninspiring it sounded and how improbable it was that the
words I said, the way I said them, could prompt her into opening up. How intrusive it must feel, my voice in the room where
she was lying just wanting to be left in peace. And I realized that
irrespective of what I said, no matter how I expressed myself, I
wouldn't get a word out of her. She'd lie there just as distant, as
reticent, loyally guarding the secret, on the strict orders of her
husband no doubt, of what had happened to her.

"Regardless of what this is about," I said, noticing I had to
make an effort just to finish the sentence, "you'd be wise to tell
us what actually happened. We can protect you, should it prove
necessary. There's no telling where things might lead if information is withheld."

My appeal was risible. I knew I was quite incapable of per-
suading anybody to do anything. And I could only assume she'd
noticed this, how averse I was to pressing forward, and figured

that if she simply lay there still for long enough, then eventually I'd get up and leave.

"Does it hurt?" I asked, if for no other reason than to hear her voice. But she just shook her head slowly, still facing away, as though she could not stand the sight of me. Her head looked odd resting on the enormous white pillow, like a dried fruit. Even her hair was dry and lifeless. What was probably usually a carefully styled crown of curls and locks resembled a dead bush, with gaps in the foilage: the small head lay there, withered and obstinate, waiting for the intruder to depart.

The nurse entered, I didn't notice her, despite the fact that she was wearing clogs, until she was standing by the bedrail pointing at her wristwatch. I remembered how beautiful I had thought all the nurses were when I'd once been in the hospital as a boy, and I recalled also that feeling I'd had of my parents ruining something for me, something big I had on the go, the day they came to collect me.

Beds were lined up along the entire length of one side of the corridor outside. On the wall, large powdery wounds were visible where the plaster had come loose. People came and went, yet a strange silence prevailed.

A doctor was standing by an empty bed holding a ring binder to his chest, looking like he was considering lying down himself. I walked over to him, something told me he was the one who had attended to Mrs. Gunerius, which indeed turned out to be the case. I asked him why he had decided to report it. The question seemed to insult him.

"Well, what kind of accident could cause those type of injuries, can you tell me that?"

I told him I could not.

Then I enquired as to why he had waited so long before notifying the authorities.

The question did not make him any more kindly disposed towards me. He began leafing through his journal, alternating

between looking at it and at the empty bed, as though the
patient would turn up as soon as he located him or her in his
papers. Then he glanced at me again, irritated by the fact I was
still there.

"The lacerations aren't consistent with a sudden, inadvertent
action. Firstly, they were made in different directions. Secondly,
they seem to have been made by a slow cutting movement, from
different points, back and forth, like so."

He performed a sawing motion with his hand.

Then he looked at me, searchingly. For a moment he seemed
more obliging, fired up perhaps by the reaction he thought he
had provoked.

He smiled, eschewing any intent to make it appear friendly.

"If I might be excused?"

His peculiar choice of words took me by surprise. He took
advantage of my momentary confusion to elbow his way past:
it was only then I realized that I had him hemmed in between
two beds.

Before leaving he said: "If you want my opinion, somebody
really took their time with her, first one leg, then the other. Who
knows, perhaps they meant to cut them right off."

He began walking away but turned once more.

"An ordinary breadknife, that's my guess."

I made my way towards the exit. An elderly man wearing a
green gown sat up from his bed with a jerk as I passed.

"Olav?" he called out. "Have you heard anything from that
Olav fellow?"

Then he laughed and reached his hand out to me. The door
at the end of the corridor opened, a woman and a little girl came
walking towards me. They seemed anxious, as though they'd
had some troubling news and feared the confirmation they had
come to receive. The girl stared at me, if I didn't know better I
would have said she thought it was my fault.

When I got outside the main entrance I turned and looked at the rows of gray opaque windows, which divulged nothing of what was going on inside. I thought about the vast number of illnesses concealed behind them, all the different ailments and all the anxieties connected to each and every one of them, the people gathered around each patient, who at this very moment was tortured by thoughts of what the worst possible outcome might be. And I pictured how one could walk from room to room, constantly being presented with something more serious, something more critical, something even more life-threatening or fatal. In this way, I thought, one could wander through the building, gradually losing all sense of care and compassion for most of the people there, as each new patient was worse off than the last and the next one would be in even poorer shape again. For each new room, a new case in even worse condition, nullifying all sympathy for the previous individual. And eventually, I thought, irrespective of whether one had been to see one hundred patients or one thousand and listened just as attentively to all, there would still be only a select few one would feel any real pity for, all compassion reserved for the very last ones, the very worst cases.

I received a text message as I was on the subway. *When you get a second? Inger.* The fact she had got hold of my mobile number didn't bother me in the slightest; on the contrary, I felt in high spirits as I replied to let her know I could come by right away, if it wasn't inconvenient.

As I was just about to press the buzzer on the outside of the building I noticed a basement window; there was a stairway leading from a gate in the railings that I also hadn't noticed before, going down to a tiny outdoor area half a story below street level. A trash can and some pots with withered flowers were standing there, and in the corner, hidden from view unless one leaned over the railings, was a door with a small window in it. It was dark behind the glass in the door but a faint yellow light shone from beneath the awning over the basement window.

I put my hand on the gate and it swung open. I descended the steps, then pressed my face to the window, placing my hands on either side of my head to shade my view. The glass was misted up but it was still possible to see in. It was a living room, furnished in an old-fashioned style: family photos on the walls, a fireplace, a wall clock, a low coffee table, two chairs, and a sofa. There was a decorated Christmas tree in one corner and a man sitting in one of the chairs. He was naked, with his legs apart, eyes closed, mouth wide open, and one hand on each armrest, as though he were about to get to his feet. Something was dangling from his ear, a string with something resembling a snail shell at the end.

When I got upstairs to Inger, I asked if she knew anything about the basement apartment. She thought it might be the superintendent's place. Then she was uncertain as to whether or not there was a super in the building, she couldn't remember having seen one in all the years she had lived there.

She corrected herself afterwards, revising her *I* into a *we*.

A computer monitor was on in the adjoining room, I could see the blue glow through the gap in the doorway. She asked me to accompany her and opened the door to the room, which turned out to be a bedroom and otherwise lay in darkness. The curtains were drawn and the little screen provided the only light. Two folding chairs were placed in front of a small desk in the corner. Why two? Was one of them meant for me? Had she arranged it prior to my arrival, made everything ready? She sat down and pulled the other chair a little closer. I looked around. The sight of the unmade bed flustered me a little, but she didn't seem to give a thought to where we were. I sat down. The room smelled of her, a slightly sweet scent. Sleep. Her sleep. Her body, tossing and turning on the sheet each night. Fragments of sleep. Dreams lasting a few seconds, just as awful as her waking thoughts. Or worse. Or perhaps there were no dreams. Just smatterings of sleep, bereft of thoughts and dreams.

"Here it is," she said.

She had put her hair into a bun, her neck shone in the light, illuminating short, fine, fair hairs growing on the nape.

There was a bird's-eye view drawing of a maze on the screen, and in the center a sparkling diamond revolved around its own axis, rendered in what, from my limited knowledge of the subject, appeared to be pretty advanced graphics. Above the labyrinth, *Demons Arise!* was written in lettering that looked like melted candle wax, and below that, in glowing font that only became visible when Inger moved the cursor over a pentagram, which was also swirling round and round, it read, *Join the quest for Haalgaard's Eye.*

"This is the game they were so into," she said.

She clicked on the writing and the maze suddenly opened: we were sucked down into it and sent barreling along through the corridors.

"They?" I said. "Were there other friends of hers who played it?"

"I don't know. I don't think so. Nobody she was friendly with from before. Just people she got to know through the game."

The mad dash through the maze came to a halt in front of a door with glinting forged nails and some grim-looking, cross-shaped iron mountings. *Log in,* it said beneath the keyhole. Inger clicked, a box popped up with space for a username and password.

"I've tried logging in," she said, "but I can't get on, I don't know, it seems they won't allow a new user as long as there's an existing one on the same computer. And I've no idea what Maria's username or password are. Do you know them, do the police?"

"What I do know," I said, "is that the ones who worked the case before have been in and checked."

"Suppose he's in there," she said. "Imagine he's behind that door, the man who took Maria."

"They examined every aspect of that game, I know that too, and they didn't turn up anything."

"How can they be sure? After all, everyone who plays it is anonymous. I know that Maria chatted online with some of them. And I mean, it could be anyone at all, and suppose she agreed to hook up with one of them, someone she only knows by some kind of Lord of the Rings name, and then went along to meet him without any clue as to what kind of person he is!"

"They have ways of looking into it," I said, "that leave them in no doubt. People online leave traces everywhere. It's possible to see who's made contact with whom. I know for a fact they've checked it out and haven't come up with anything."

She brought the little white arrow over the rough wooden planks in the door and clicked several times, as though she believed she'd find her, somewhere or other in the maze, if only the damned door would open.

I thought about it for a moment then placed my hand on her shoulder, just below the downy, delicate hairs.

"It's not one of them," I said. "It's got nothing to do with that game."

She stopped clicking on the mouse.

It was impossible to know whether or not my hand bothered her.

"There's no point," I said. "Maria isn't there."

I felt a sensation in my chest as I said it, without understanding why, not for a moment afterwards: it was the first time I had said her name aloud.

I removed my hand. She turned and looked at me, I didn't know how I was supposed to perceive the look she gave me, nor could I manage to meet it, so I glanced back at the screen instead and stared at the cursor, now an immobile pointed finger on the keyhole. I was aware of her still looking at me. I thought about the bed behind us, just a few meters away. I tried to think of something else, attempted to picture Mrs. Gunerius, lying with her legs raised, silent as to how she had come to be in that wretched situation. I tried to remember why I was there, but it was futile, the only thing I could have expected to achieve, it dawned on me, was exactly this, to get her hopes up, to further strengthen the impression that something was being done, that the case was being worked on, that something was going to happen, and in so doing, I thought, further enhance the unpleasantness and difficulty, the rage and despair on the day she realized, yet again, that nothing had happened, nothing had been done, nothing could be done beyond what already had been or been attempted.

I smoked two cigarettes in the time it took me to walk to the supermarket. It was only after I had gone some distance that I noticed that it had stopped raining. It had been so long since it hadn't been bucketing down that it felt criminal to stroll along like this without covering up. But the sky was like a sponge. The slightest pressure and it would pour down. It was wet everywhere, as though the city had just risen up from the sea.

While I was in the store it started to rain again. It lashed against the large windowpanes and the special-offer signs on the pavement bent backwards. The girl at the checkout was called Chantal, and according to her nametag was a trainee. She was nervous, gave a little sigh of relief every time there was a beep. I pictured her with her throat slit from ear to ear. Chantal (23).

Anne-Sofie was in the doorway when I stepped out of the elevator. She didn't reply when I said hello, just stood there, blocking my path. In the end I had to ask her to move. At which point she pushed the door open but remained where she was. I went in and heard the clunk of the door as it came back into her body.

"Where have you been?" she asked.

"I've been working," I replied, trying to remove my shoes quickly but the laces were soaking and the sodden knots impossible to untie.

"Been working," she mimicked. "I see. I notice you don't say you've *been at work*, but that you've *been working*. Let me put it another way. Where have you been working?"

"I've been at the office," I said. "I have a mountain of paperwork to get through."

I finally managed to loosen the knot on the second shoe and could pull my foot free. I picked up the shopping bags and went into the kitchen. It was like a steam room in there, the windows were completely fogged up. There was a saucepan on the stove with the heat on full, I turned off the burner and took the saucepan off, it sizzled.

"You need to be more careful!" I called out.

I began taking the groceries out of the bags.

"That could have been dangerous!" I continued, unsure of where exactly she was. I crumpled up the bags and tossed them in to the cupboard beneath the countertop.

"Are you sleeping with her?" I heard from behind me.

I turned.

"What do you mean?" I asked, as calmly as I was able.

She laughed.

"What do I mean?" Her voice was completely distorted. "Surely what I mean is pretty obvious. It's not that hard to understand, is it? I'm asking you if you're sleeping with her. And you're acting as if you don't have a clue what I'm talking about. Interesting. Is that because you need time to come up with something? Is it? Is that what you're up to now, Kristian, are you racking your brain, trying to think of something to say, something that won't give you away?"

"Anne," I said. "I can't . . . I can't deal with this, not right now."

"When can you deal with it then? When will you be able to give me a simple answer? You do remember what I asked you, don't you? I asked you if you were sleeping with her."

She gesticulated with her arms.

"So when do you think you'll be ready to provide me with an answer? It's not demanding too much to want to know, is it? It's not like I'm asking you to address the UN Security Council, now is it? A yes or no will suffice."

"No," I said and noticed how hard it was for me to say it. "I'm not sleeping with her."

"There you go," she said, in a softer tone. "That wasn't so difficult now, was it?"

She turned and left.

"But that doesn't mean I'm not going to!" I called out after her.

I stood waiting for her to reappear in the doorway, certain she would come back. But as the seconds ticked by and she didn't return, it was as though she were no longer there, as if she had left the apartment, no matter how unlikely I knew that to be: there wasn't a sound to be heard. Then I got it into my head that she was in the hallway, just outside the kitchen door, listening. The longer I stood there, the stronger the feeling of her being there, being somewhere very close by.

"She is a lovely looking woman," I said, but not too loudly, I figured if she was not there, like I thought, then she would come when she heard me, that she'd be unable to resist popping back in order to hear what I said.

"Horny as hell," I said. "I could tell that from the start."

I listened, strained my ears to hear if she was there.

"As soon as she gets over losing that stupid kid, she'll be ripe for some cock, I'm pretty sure of that."

I looked at the window, it wasn't misted up anymore, but it was raining outside, everything merging into one in the pane.

"Honey?"

I heard the distant sound of a siren, footsteps in the apartment above and a rumbling from my stomach, I couldn't remember the last time I ate, I suddenly felt completely empty, as though something were whirling around inside me looking for a toehold but finding none.

"Honey?" I repeated. "Are you there?"

The case with the Korean gang had been the worst yet. The more Bernhard and I got tangled up in it, the more baffling it became. Two prostitutes and a policeman wound up dead before it was over. And we never actually got hold of the guy who did it, I'm certain of that. We would have been better off charging the first guy who came along, the chances of it being our man would have been about the same. That was how it felt a lot of the time. Like we were the ones who brought the chaos, introduced it where a careful arrangement had been in place, a meticulous and detailed order had reigned, insanely complicated, invisible and incomprehensible. But it was there. It held sway until we came along and disrupted everything. That was what we did, we ushered disorder into the preexisting system, the structure already in place that would have led us straight to the solution if we had only known beforehand where to place our feet, step by step. Already, from the moment we had formed an initial theory of what had happened we had messed things up, taken the wrong turn. A successful investigation was one where we eventually managed to disentangle ourselves from our own erroneous deductions and the reasoning that led us away from what was clear as day before we got started on it.

It was the same feeling I got as I walked into Gunerius's office. Here it is, everything right in front of me, I thought, stretched out like a delicate web. From now on I can only botch it up.

I had to admit, begrudgingly, that the man the press constantly referred to as the Hotel King did actually resemble one, seated there in a high-backed chair, carved-wood onion domes flanking either side of his broad face. Above him, in an enormous gold frame, hung a painting in the National Romantic style, and even though it was, as far as I could judge, an outstanding example of the genre, he may as well have just written a sign with twenty million on it and hung it there instead. There were objets d'art and artifacts all around the room, sculptures both large and small, gilded pitchers and bowls, deer antlers, a stuffed pine marten, an African shield, a Russian samovar.

Gunerius himself looked as though his form had been pressed down into the chair by force. He sat with his arms on the desk, his hands glistening with sweat, and his fingers so fat they splayed apart.

I thought about the little head lying on the hospital pillow.

"Wold?" he said. "What's this about?"

He stared at me as if hoping for a reaction, astonished admiration, awe perhaps, some sign of being overwhelmed at the extravagance of his office, more than expecting an explanation of my visit. Hadn't he understood that it concerned his wife, or was he just pretending not to?

"Your wife's accident," I said.

"What about it?" he asked, with a contempt I imagined I would have encountered anyway: he was the kind of person who was hard and hateful to the world in general and whose driving force behind his own success was revenge, revenge on all those who had believed he wouldn't amount to much. I wondered who it was that had put the idea in his head. A nasty teacher? Some friends who had bullied him for being fat? A girl who had laughed at him the first time he had made advances? He reminded me of the men behind the Krakow affair, who had built up a little empire of brothels in the old Eastern Bloc, none of the girls over twenty: his fingers glistened in the same way, as though covered in grease.

"We're not quite sure what to make of it," I said, and felt an intense desire to disrupt his plans, make things difficult for him, throw a wrench in the works.

"What on earth makes you think you have any right to

make anything at all of it?" Gunerius said, taking hold of both armrests, looking as though he wanted to get to his feet, but abandoning the effort when he remembered how heavy he was.

"We wonder whether there could be something else behind the accident than what was previously claimed."

I had not planned on being so direct, but suddenly felt at a loss, uncertain, like a rookie, as though his office and decor had had the effect on me it was presumably intended to have on all who entered. I felt like a tenant farmer, stooping in front of the lord of the manor's mahogany.

"We feel there are some questionable aspects about how it came about and we'll be taking a closer look at it."

Gunerius snorted. "Questionable aspects? No more questionable than how incompetent that imbecile of a gardener can be. Who, incidentally, has been fired, and is probably sitting on the train back to Vilnius at this very moment."

"Do you have a number for him?"

"No! And I count myself lucky I don't. I hope for his own sake he never gets the opportunity of getting his hands on any power tools again."

"Were you there when it happened?"

"No."

"Was there anybody else present who can confirm it?"

"Listen here, my dear fellow, my wife was present, the poor thing, and she has explained what needs explaining. So I don't understand what reason you could have for spending any more time on this?"

"We investigate everything where the circumstances could be viewed as in any way suspicious."

Gunerius looked at me, as if gauging how much opposition he could expect on my part. Then, after what seemed to me careful consideration, he said: "What's the name of your superior?"

"It was my superior who requested me to take a look at the case."

"And now you have taken a look," he said, derisively, "and I trust you've seen that there is nothing you need concern yourself with, which you can now report back to your superior."

The fact that he seemed so unaffected by his wife having to spend the rest of her life as an invalid: was this manner something other than the natural professional distance he displayed to someone with whom he wanted to limit his dealings to an absolute minimum? I hadn't noticed how little it seemed to trouble him, not before he said *poor thing*. It was completely out of place. It didn't sound like it came from him, more like he had stolen the expression from somebody else. Why did he say it? Why insert it? Why bother in front of me? What did he have to prove, to me, to anyone? I thought back to one of the stories I'd heard about him, one everyone knew, which had appeared in an unauthorized biography, where an inebriated Gunerius had dragged out a meeting with a foreign hotel chain about a huge contract for several hours, before finally grabbing the negotiator between the legs and yelling into his ear, wanting to know if it wasn't time to get some signatures down on paper.

I took out my cigarettes. "May I smoke?"

"No, you may not."

I followed his eyes. An ashtray with a figurine on it lay on the desk beside a penholder.

I paused, then I asked: "How long have you been married?"

Gunerius looked like he didn't believe what he was hearing. His sausage fingers grabbed hold of a pen.

"The name of your superior was . . ."

"Are you involved in any conflicts at the moment, is there anyone who might wish to get at you by harming your wife?"

"That would take my secretary five minutes to find out."

"Because I think it would be natural," I continued, "to assume that it was you that they were out to get?"

Gunerius pressed a button.

"Can you put me through to the chief of police?"

A crackly voice responded.

"The chief of police!" he roared. "I don't fucking know what kind of titles the lot of them have!"

"In any case, it would be of help," I said, "if you could provide us with the names of anyone who may have a score to settle and could conceivably go to such drastic lengths."

Gunerius continued to hold the button down.

"And Else, could you show the inspector out? We're finished now."

As the secretary escorted me to the elevator, I thought about how he had seemed to swell and fill up the chair even more in the time I had spent in the office, and I wondered if I would have been quite so forward if I hadn't got it into my head that he was stuck, that he wouldn't have been able to get to his feet no matter how much he might have wanted to.

The car was Bernhard's idea. He thought it would help us get close to Sahid, who Bernhard had convinced me was behind the failed robbery of the cash transport in February, where one of the guards had been killed. Bernhard stuck his head under the hood for five minutes, then towed me up to Sahid's garage. Two days later one of our informants gave us everything we needed to know, so I could have saved myself the bother, and I didn't know if it was because our ploy had been exposed, but every time I called up about the car the waiting time kept increasing by a couple of days.

It was wet everywhere, all the same I walked in a zigzag, as though my feet could not help seeking out the spots where the tarmac appeared driest. There were puddles all over, greasy with oil, a bottle floated in one and if a genie had emerged I would have wished for a dry pair of socks. In the sky above the terraced house where Halvard Vendelbo lived, a charcoal-gray cloud had formed, resembling a duvet. A pile of trash bags lay on the pavement. Crows had pecked a hole in one of them and gorged themselves on some indeterminate contents that littered a large area around.

I dropped my cigarette in a puddle, it extinguished with a hiss. I had a long wait between my ringing the doorbell and him opening, and even then he tarried as long as he could before letting me in, as if hoping right to the end that it would not be necessary. When I called him on the phone he had made no attempt to hide what a bad idea he thought it was, how unable he was to understand my reasoning and how little faith he had in my motivations in relation to the case. I couldn't blame him, nor could I count on things improving much when I was face to face with him and stated the grounds anew.

We stood in the hallway. For the moment he showed no indication of letting me in any further.

"I don't understand why this is necessary," he half-wheezed, half-whispered. "Don't you all have anything else to do other than talk to us? Wouldn't you be better off using the time to search for Maria instead?"

I wanted to say something but didn't know what, fortunately he just continued talking.

"Maria is dead. Surely you realize that? I know Inger hasn't but I have, and I have to presume the police have as well, so why Inger and I have to sit answering questions we've answered a hundred times before, it's . . . it's . . . it's . . ."

He was right up in my face. I clenched one fist.

"For fuck's sake!"

He took a step back.

"Don't you understand that nothing comes of this, nothing other than more misery? Inger and I have to deal with the whole thing all over again, while you, you get nothing. Don't you get that? What is it you actually imagine you'll find out that you don't know from before?"

A noise came from one of the rooms and he composed himself. With a gesture, as though the conversation hadn't taken place, as though he just opened the door to me, he showed me into the living room.

There was a fire burning. Almost everything in the room was white, the walls, the shelves, the sofa and chairs, even the fireplace was white, with a textured finish of small pointed nubbles. A woman was just getting to her feet to nudge the fireguard back into place.

"Kristina," Vendelbo said.

She nodded.

I put out my hand.

"Kristian," I said, and although I had intended to say something more, the similarity in our names, which I hadn't considered before, made me stop.

She laughed. It took Vendelbo a while to realize why and then he too began to laugh, and then I couldn't help but join in.

We stood laughing out loud, all three of us. Kristina held her hand to her midriff. Afterwards, when she'd dried the tears from her face, she left her hand on top of her stomach.

I noticed Vendelbo looking at me.

"He's the one leading the investigation now," he said, his eyes still fixed on me, as though to emphasize something. "He's come to inform us of the latest developments."

Kristina looked at him.

"No, there's nothing new," Vendelbo said. "Just an update, as far I can gather, of what's been done and how they'll proceed."

He smiled, his lips pressed together.

She returned the smile, then left.

"Life goes on," he said, as an explanation of sorts, as soon as she was gone: it struck me that that was the real reason he didn't want me coming around, he didn't want me to know he was going to be a father again.

"We can't spend the rest of our lives waiting. Who benefits from that? Not us, at any rate. Not Maria either."

We sat down. His skin had the same kind of wan look as Inger's, I saw that now, but it didn't pervade his face the way it did Inger's, the grayness wasn't as deep.

"I wish Inger could recognize that too," he said.

I pictured him together with her, the night he'd been there and they'd made love, I saw the two grieving parents in each other's arms, passion catching them off guard, like some grotesque memory of the time before deep sorrow existed: the groans and cries of arousal which, for a short time, drowned it out.

"Maria is gone," he said. "Some sick bastard took her. And now she's dead."

He seemed so cocksure, sitting there. It bordered on provocative. But it was true: he was in the right. He was safe no matter what. He could say what he liked. Nobody can correct someone who's in mourning. He was the father of a lost child, he was fully within his rights, he could do as he liked, express, or forego expressing, the inconceivable pain in whatever way came naturally to him, no one could oppose him or demand he act any other way. He could behave exactly as he wished. He could deal with those around him at his own discretion and they could not object, they could not expect anything more of him, he could treat me like a piece of shit and I would have no choice but to indulge him, put up with whatever I was subjected to, forgive him for it, tolerate, understand, and accept it, because he was in the right, he took precedence, he had right of way over the rest of us by virtue of the tragedy that had befallen him.

"So, why are you here, exactly?"

Why on earth was I there? What more could I hope to achieve than to twist the knife, stir despair from its slumber, force him to watch the gruesome movie one more time.

I began by explaining that I was new on the case, that I had been assigned as a "fresh pair of eyes" to go through everything in the hope of discovering something new, in case there'd been any oversights, and since the case was new for me I'd decided to talk to him and Inger. Although I was well aware, I added, in an attempt to bring him slightly around, how many times they'd answered the same questions I would pose, and conscious of the very small chance of turning up something which had not been thoroughly checked out already.

While I spoke, tiredness crept over me, a reluctance to continue, as if I was utterly fatigued, due possibly, or at least to some extent, to the warmth from the fire, which was sending unbearable waves of heat into the room.

"But I don't understand what I can tell you that you haven't heard before," he said, less reproach in his tone than there might have been, had he so wished. "Surely everything is there to see, in the police material."

"There was one minor thing," I said. "It may well be of no relevance. But in one of your interviews you said that Maria wished to spend more time at your place, that she had spoken to you about living here, together with you and Kristina, and that she had also asked you about the possibility of changing schools. Is that right?"

"We didn't discuss it at any length but she did mention it a couple of times, yes."

I could see he was wary.

I had no idea how to continue the line of questioning.

"Why do you ask?"

"Because," I said, unsure of what I was going to, or ought to, say when referring to Inger.

"Because Maria's mother," I said, "didn't perceive it the same way, of that being something Maria wanted. In fact, she believed the opposite to be the case."

"What do you mean, the opposite?"

"That she was under the impression that Maria wanted to spend more time at her place."

"She'd only mentioned it in passing a couple of times, so it's hardly surprising she hadn't raised the matter with Inger, is it?"

Why did I feel a twinge when he said her name?

He shook his head.

"But I don't get . . ." he said, "what this can have to do with her disappearance."

I replied that we had every reason to assume it had nothing to do with it, that the reason I had brought it up was because part of my brief was to note any possible discrepancies in already existing statements so as to investigate if there was anything to be found in these that could provide us with a lead, and that this was just such an example, which I was obliged to discuss with him as a matter of procedure.

"You've been to see Inger," he said, I didn't know if it was a question or an assertion. "So what does she say? That Maria wanted to spend more time at her place?"

"Something along those lines," I said, making up my mind not to allow myself to be questioned any closer.

He sat looking like he was mulling things over.

"What others have you turned up?" he suddenly asked.

"Pardon?"

"What other discrepancies have you turned up?"

It was impossible to tell whether the quaver in his voice was due to unease or anger.

"Nothing else so far," I replied. "I know you've answered this before, but I need to ask you to consider one more time if you are quite sure that there can't have been a boy in the picture that neither of you were aware of?"

He threw his hands up.

"Jesus Christ! Are you all still harping on about that!"

The aggressive attitude from earlier in the hallway was back.

He took a deep breath. "Yes, I've answered the question before, and I'm telling you for the last time. Maria didn't have a boyfriend. If she had, I would have known about it. I would have known about it and Inger would have known about it."

"There are many cases," I said, "where the parents swear to the same thing and it turns out that their children have run off with someone they've been with for a long time, without anyone, not even their friends, knowing anything about it. They can be surprisingly cunning when it comes to hiding things like that."

"Be that as it may, I'm telling you, Maria didn't have a boyfriend. Inger will say the same thing. If she hasn't already."

Again the self-assurance, almost bordering on arrogance, and this time it annoyed me. I wanted to scare him, take him down a peg or two, bring him back down to earth, return him to the depths of despair. He should be sitting there worn out, eyes red from crying, instead of looking so smug. I knew I could manage it if I wanted to. I knew that a few well-chosen words could, within the space of a few minutes, or just a few seconds, reduce him to a nervous wreck.

I considered giving him the impression that I had something

on him, that it might be possible that we would need to bring him back in for questioning. Wring a little more humility out of him, render him more amenable, by intimating that I could easily concentrate my interest on his role in the disappearance. I would have liked to see how long he could manage to keep his cool then, before giving in to either rage or despair.

"What about *Demons Arise*?" I asked.

"What about it?"

"Were you aware that she was spending time playing that?"

It took him such a long time to answer that when he finally did it wasn't necessary.

"Like I told you," I said. "It's very rare for the parents not to be surprised about what eventually comes out."

For the first time since I had been there I sensed I had the upper hand. It felt good.

I continued: "So you see, that's why we have to ask about everything, put the same questions to you again, keep all options open, no matter how sure you are, and no matter how good your reasons are for being so."

I glanced around the room. There were no curtains, just a large amount of plants in all shapes and sizes distributed over several stories of white shelving across the windows. The living room was otherwise devoid of objects, no newspapers or magazines, no cups or cigarettes. As though they, the two of them, didn't do anything in there apart from sit stock-still in the chairs.

"So, are we finished?" Vendelbo asked.

"How did you react when you heard about her disappearance?" I asked.

"Am I supposed to take this seriously?" he replied, quite calmly.

"What was your first thought, when you heard she was missing?" I went on, even though I knew he was the one that would emerge victorious.

"The first thought I had," he said in a low tone, "was that considering how incompetent the police are in this country, we'd probably have to face the fact she'd never be found."

I didn't know how to respond. If I continued on with my line of questioning he would just steer things where he wanted. Defeat was a fact. I had gone too far and paid for it.

"Do you have any photographs of Maria?" I asked.

"No," he said.

He stared at me defiantly, as though waiting for any excuse to hit me.

"We all have our ways of dealing with grief," he said after a while, like a response to what he knew I wanted to confront him with. "You'd no doubt act differently, if you were in my position. I do it my way. And if there isn't anything else, I'd like you to leave. I have . . ."

He didn't say any more, but nodded in the direction of a doorway, which I assumed led into the kitchen.

We got to our feet. His girlfriend appeared, holding a carafe from a coffee maker.

"Are you leaving already?" she asked, a slightly concerned look on her face. She appeared completely different now to when we had been introduced: she'd seemed carefree and happy then, as though, I thought, she hadn't been aware of Maria.

"Everything's fine, dear," Vendelbo said. "Wold needs to be heading out."

She remained standing, leaning against the door frame, the carafe in her hand: her pitiful appearance and the assertive hand placed on my shoulder gave me the sense of something unwholesome about the household.

He grabbed my arm as I was opening the front door.

"If this is all the police have to come up with . . ." He hesitated slightly. "Then I'd rather you just kept it to yourselves and didn't keep us apprised. You're just adding insult to injury. You understand? Send word the day you actually find her. Until then

I don't want to know anything about what you're up to. I only want to know if you find her. Okay?"

I made no reply.

"And I think the same should go for Inger. Things are difficult enough for her as it is, without you guys banging on the door every five minutes again."

I walked out into the rain, the first few drops on my hair felt refreshing, my lungs drew the moist air in with relish, I felt damp all through, as if I hadn't been indoors long enough to dry off properly.

Vendelbo yelled after me.

I turned. He was standing on the stoop.

"Drop it," he called out. "This isn't doing anybody any good!"

The rain crackled on the bushes as though on paper. In a small window about half a story above the entrance, it must have been the turn on the stairs to the second floor, I saw a face, or something resembling a face. At first I was unsure what it was, a curtain or a section of the wall behind, but it suddenly moved. I thought of the unborn child. It made me shudder, as though the only future it had in store was also to suddenly disappear in fourteen years.

Anne-Sofie called my mobile just as Inger was opening the door.

"Where are you?" she asked.

I looked at Inger, she turned and walked back into the living room.

"I'm at the office," I said.

"I just called there," she said.

"I'm down in the archives."

It just came out, I hardly needed to think before speaking.

It went quiet on the other end of the line.

"When will you be home?"

"Dunno. I'll ring you in a little while, okay?"

Silence. I could hear her breathing. Or was she crying? It sounded like sobbing.

"Okay?" I repeated, but I knew she wouldn't answer.

I hung up and turned off the mobile. When I got into the living room Inger had already put out a tray with two glasses and some bottles of mineral water and beer.

"Are you driving?"

"Car's in for repairs. Should be ready in a day or two."

She opened the beer, apparently interpreting that as the consequence of my answer.

"Not something I'm used to," I said, "public transport."

The casual tone with which I said it felt strange. It was like I was there for other reasons than Maria. I took a sip of beer. It tasted refreshing, the bubbly bitterness circulating throughout. I wanted to say something, would have liked to sustain the laid-back tone, but could not think of anything.

"What's wrong with your wife?" she asked.

"What do you mean?"

"You seem worried."

I didn't have the energy to respond.

"It's like you're scared of something happening," she said, after a while. "Of something happening to her."

And then, after yet another pause: "Or scared of her, perhaps."

It sounded like she was sitting far away when she spoke. I pondered how if I answered then something would come loose, or split apart and it would prove impossible to put it back together afterwards. I drank a little more, felt myself growing slightly tipsy.

"Is she ill?"

I nodded.

"Is it serious?"

I shrugged, felt a sudden juvenile embarrassment, and noticed how striking her lips were, how they didn't seem to blend in with the rest of her features anymore.

"They don't know what it is," I said. "She's taken all kinds of tests. Still they can't figure it out. Nothing seems to help."

"But what is it that . . . ?"

I interrupted her: "It's impossible to say where one thing ends and the other begins. I don't understand it. Neither do the doctors. She doesn't even understand it herself."

We sat for a while in silence. Inger topped off my glass.

"What's her name?"

I wanted to answer but couldn't bring myself to do it.

I said: "It's like she's staring into darkness the whole time. As though she's not able to look away."

"When did it start?"

Her voice, the calmness of it, and the effortless way she posed questions gave me a tingling sensation. All I wanted was to be there, close to her, listen to her voice and talk to her.

"Tell me about Maria," I said.

She gave me a slightly confused look.

"What do you want to know?"

"No, not like that," I said. "Just tell me about her. What she was like."

She sat staring for a long time, trying to bring something to mind.

Then she smiled.

"She looked terrible when she was born. Her nose was here and her mouth was over there . . ." she said, pointing. "One eye was completely glued shut. She looked like she'd gone seven rounds in the ring."

We laughed.

"She was sick a lot when she was small. Couldn't keep food down. Got thinner and thinner no matter what we tried to fill her up with. Halvard . . ."

She hesitated, uncertain as to whether or not she should bring him up.

"Halvard was beside himself with worry. Fed her corn oil. Stuffed her full of crisps. Tried everything. It went on like that for years. Then one day she just got over it. Suddenly everything was how it should be. No more problems at all.

"But it was weird," she said. "There was something strange about it. As though . . . I don't know how to put it. But it was as if he didn't like the fact that Maria was well. I'm aware of how that sounds . . . and that's not how it was, either. But it was like he, yeah, like he lost interest in her, seeing as he didn't need to be so concerned about her any longer. I noticed it in both of them. Even though the two of them had been so . . ."

She hooked one index finger around the other.

"As though he'd lost whatever it was that held them together."

She shook her head.

"Maybe it just seemed that way. I don't know. I'm not sure. I brought it up once, I probably shouldn't have, that only made things worse, made him withdraw even further. More and more was left up to me. Dropping her off to school or to friends and collecting her. Parent-teacher meetings. Training and sports

meets. More and more of just me and her, and him on his own.
That was when we started to drift apart, I think, that was the
beginning of the end for us, when Maria got better. In a way,
they were the best years we had together, all that time she was
ill, when we were out of our minds with worry and didn't know
what to do to help her."

A tear ran down her cheek, coming to rest at the corner of
her mouth.

"Since then, everything's just been . . . a mess. As if we didn't
know one another. As if we'd also lost whatever it was that kept
us together."

"What about Maria?" I asked. "How did she take it?"

"For a few years," she said, the tears had left a dried-up rill
running from each eye, "everything was . . . normal. She had
friends, seemed happy. Played sports. Was enthusiastic about
everything she was involved in. Then she started secondary
school and it was like she changed completely. More than you'd
expect, I mean. I figured it was me and Halvard who were to
blame, first all the arguing and then the breakup."

"In what way did she change?"

"She packed in everything. Wouldn't take part in anything,
not sports, not dance, nothing. Became withdrawn. It was
impossible to get a word out of her. She never smiled. Never
laughed. Never asked about anything. Never told us anything.
But most of all she just . . . seemed so sad. So profoundly sad.
As though there wasn't room for any other feelings inside her."

She looked at me. I wanted to go over to her, I knew she'd
let me, allow me to put my arms around her, allow me to pull
her close.

"That was the first thing I thought of when she disappeared,
not that she'd been kidnapped, but that she'd taken her own
life."

"Did she ever talk about that?"

"Never."

She smiled.

"But then again she never talked about anything!"

Her lips began to quiver.

"I scolded her the day she disappeared. The last thing I did was to tell her off. I haven't told anybody that. Should I have?"

She looked at me.

"I was so fed up with her moaning! The only time she said anything was when she was dissatisfied with something. When she opened her mouth it was only to complain. To grumble and groan. It was the same that evening. She hadn't said anything all day. And then she suddenly came into the bathroom while I was having a shower and started going on at me for forgetting to buy milk. And then I told her off and said . . ."

Her voice trailed off into a hoarse chirp, as though snapping in two.

"And said she could take some money and go to the shop herself."

She cleared her throat.

"Should I have told them? I didn't dare to mention it. I was afraid that . . . I don't know what I was afraid of. But I didn't dare say it. Do you think I should have?"

I didn't say anything, just shook my head slowly.

She got up and walked over to the window.

"That was the last thing she heard me say, that I was sick of her moaning, fed up with being at her beck and call and that she could look after herself from now on."

The rain was pouring down. I had a fleeting notion of the deluge having taken her and of her being found on the first day the sun shone.

Inger stood with her back to me.

"I think I know," she said after a long time, "why you only come here in the early evening."

She turned.

"What do you mean?"

She looked at me.

"You come here when you're finished for the day, don't you?"

I didn't reply.

"The others, the rest of your colleagues, they don't know you're here. Because you're not meant to be. You're not meant to do anything. There's nothing more that's supposed to happen with this case, that's why you got it. The rest of them are finished with it. They've got other things to do."

"It's not quite the way you describe it."

"But pretty much," she retorted. "And you've probably got other cases as well, more pressing ones than this. You work on them during office hours. That's why you don't come around then. You're not allowed. This case is getting so old that you're not permitted to use time or resources on it."

She fixed me with a harsh stare. "You were only assigned to it because they need someone to be formally responsible for it."

"That's not correct," I said.

"But why did they put you on the case? Why not one of those who'd already worked on it? What was the point of bringing in someone completely new?"

"To look at it with a fresh pair of eyes. Since the others couldn't make any progress. To see if it was possible that thinking about things in a different way could lead to anything new."

"Yeah? And can it? Is it possible to think it through in a new way? Haven't they already tried everything a hundred times?"

"I don't know. I honestly don't know, and I won't know before I've been through all the material. But that takes time. Just getting through it all takes a lot of time. There's an enormous amount. It takes time to collate. But I'm working hard at it. And I won't give up until I've been through everything. If there is something there, I'll find it. I promise."

Finally I understood. She herself had stopped hoping. She had given up, had been aware for some time that we were not going to find her, and that if we did, she would be dead. The waiting, the searching, the clinging on to hope had been just as much an act on her part as it had been for the investigators. That was why she had been so angry the first time I came by, because I served to remind her that that was something she could not permit herself. There was something shocking about it, something immoral. If anyone was obliged to keep hope alive, then it was her, the mother. She was the one who was never supposed to give up. Her immutable mandate was to make sure the colors of hope surged through uncertainty, up until certainty came to pass. Until then, until the day somebody showed her her daughter's mortal remains, she was to be the rock, the power holding on tight to the possibility of Maria turning up at any moment and rushing towards her with arms outstretched.

I went over to where she was standing. I hesitated for a second, then put my arms around her. She succumbed. Her whole body convulsed. To my horror, I noticed I had an erection. She cried, her tears running into the hollow at the base of my throat. Then she raised her head, wiped her eyes, and looked at me, before stretching her neck and lifting her chin. I bent over her and we kissed. My cock was pressing against her stomach, it felt like I could lift her up and carry her on it through the room if I wanted to, and she could feel it, she must have been able to feel it, and still she held me and would not let go, we clung on tightly to each other and would not let go, neither of us.

2

Everything was quiet, nothing stirred, from now on every movement could be carried out with the same degree of calm. I brought the cigarette slowly to my mouth and let my hand fall away gradually, took a drag and held it for a long time before releasing. I tapped the ash into an eggcup she had found for me that I held in my hand. It was white porcelain with a little blue landscape painted on it, featuring a tavern, some trees, and a stone bridge arching over a stream. The wind blew, the curtains moved, and on the floor by the window a small puddle had formed. I felt her foot pressing against my thigh. I turned. She was lying on her front with her hands under her head and the duvet just below her behind. She looked peaceful. I placed my hand between her shoulders before sliding it to the small of her back, where the downy hair was slightly denser, and then all the way over her buttocks, which quivered slightly when I let go of them. She was soft all over, my hand met no resistance.

I stubbed out the cigarette and lay down, putting my leg and arm over her. When I found her hand I wrapped my fingers through hers and held tight. Her hair smelled of fresh sweat.

"Inger," I whispered.

No response.

I did not want to say it but I had to all the same.

"I need to go soon."

No reply this time either, but my fingers felt a hard squeeze.

A few moments later when I tried to wiggle my hand free, she let out a groan and pulled me back over her. I rested my cheek on her shoulder blade, which was like a saucer.

After that I don't know whether an hour passed by or only a few minutes.

"Why do you always have to leave?"

She turned around, our bodies separating with a sticky sound. We lay on our backs, faces turned to one another, her expression was indeterminate, almost neutral: it conveyed nothing.

"Why is it always like this? Why isn't it possible to be in one place without thinking of something somewhere else?"

"I don't know," I said.

I propped myself up on my elbows and leaned over her. At first she lay quite still and let me kiss her. Then she opened up and let me in.

A gust of wind swept through the room, slamming the door to the living room. We both awoke with a gasp. I pulled her close, said "Hush," and stroked her hair. Her nails dug into my skin. We were sweaty, I inhaled her smell, felt like I could never get enough of it.

"I was dreaming," she mumbled. "I was dreaming something."

She felt tense in my arms, like she was ready to jump.

"I can't remember what. Something about . . . No, it's gone."

The tension diminished, her body grew heavier and relaxed in my embrace.

"It's so strange," she said. "How is it we never realize it's a dream? Why do we believe it every time?"

There were noises from down on the street, a woman screamed, some men began to quarrel, then a clatter and the sound of a window being smashed. Several voices began to mingle, resounding as though in a huge hall, then faded away.

"Dreams are the only things we never learn to see through," Inger said.

In the calm after the scuffle on the street, the heavens took the opportunity to open up again, splattering rain on the windowsill.

"I never dream," I said.

"That I don't believe," she replied.

"It's true. I never dream. I can't remember a single one I've had."

"Then that's all it is, the fact you don't recall them."

"When we were asleep just now . . ."

"You were dreaming then," she interrupted. "We lay here dreaming, both of us. Two different worlds, one head against the other."

I wanted to disagree but let it go, was enjoying the back and forth too much.

I pressed my nose into her hair.

"I never used to dream about her before," she said. "When she was small she was never in my dreams. Never. I dreamed about everyone I knew, except Maria. I couldn't understand why. It was like she no longer existed when I slept. I felt bad about it at first. Thought maybe it was because I didn't care enough about her. That I was more concerned about everyone else. I didn't dare tell anyone either. I was ashamed. What kind of mother doesn't have room in her dreams for her daughter? I did mention it to someone in the end, not Halvard, but a friend of mine, she'd given birth around the same time as me. And she said that the opposite was probably the case, that the reason I didn't dream about her was because I didn't need to. That I felt secure. That there was nothing for me to be anxious about."

She twisted loose from my embrace.

"It sounded so reasonable when she said it. So I let it be a comfort to me. Imagined she was right."

"Wasn't she?"

"Then the changes I told you about began to occur. Maria changed. And Halvard and I . . ."

She stopped. She'd uttered his name in a strange way, had heard it herself, like the name of a person she didn't know, a name she was uncertain how to pronounce.

"I remembered what my friend had said and thought that I would surely start dreaming about her now, now that I was worried about her."

She gave an ironic smile.

"It was like I was lying there, each night, waiting for the proof that I actually cared."

I didn't want her to talk about Maria. Everything to do with Maria pulled her away from me, trivialized what we had.

"But still nothing. I continued dreaming about everybody else apart from her."

Her lips began to tremble.

"And now . . ."

She grabbed my arms and pressed her face into my chest.

"Now I dream about her every time I sleep!"

I held my arms around her. Then pulled back a little, enough to see her features.

But she lowered her head, hid her face.

Like Maria in the vacation pictures, I thought.

"So, what happens in these dreams you have about her?"

"Practically the same thing every time," she said after a while. "It starts off as a different dream. A normal dream. It can be about anything. And then, towards the end, she appears. She emerges from someplace or another, walks towards me with her arms like this."

She held her arms out towards me.

"And I stand there, holding her, thinking that if I just hang on long enough, then she'll never disappear again."

I was awoken by the sound of her voice.

"Be completely honest with me, Kristian," she said.

"What is it?" I replied, noticing the anxiety that had filled the room while I had slumbered.

"Will Maria be found?"

I reached out for her, didn't have the energy to open my eyes wide, didn't know what part of her body I took hold of.

"She'll be found."

"Alive? Is there any chance at all, that she's alive? Tell me the truth."

"There's a chance," I said. "There's a chance of it."

"You're just saying that," she said, but I could hear by her voice she wanted to be contradicted.

Mrs. Gunerius was sitting on the balcony in a wheelchair, smoking and looking like she had found a comfortable position for her legs, straight out and on a footrest. She didn't seem as worn out anymore, as though it had been six months since I'd visited her and not a week. The rain poured down from the projecting ledge above, forming a watery tent around us. She asked if I would like a cigarette, in a voice that was surprisingly deep, and also stern, the only sound I had been expecting from that little head of hers was something high-pitched, slight, and frail: now it sounded as though someone else had crept inside her and begun to speak. I politely declined her offer and took out my own. There was something promising about it, the two of us sitting there with a cigarette each, as if perhaps it might be possible to get something out of her after all.

"Have you thought about what I said?"

"No," she replied.

Once again I was taken aback by her voice.

"Is there any chance you might be willing to? Consider it, I mean, what I suggested?"

"No."

She had finished the cigarette and was stretching for the packet, which lay on a small table by the door, she had just about made it, but managed to give them a little nudge, sending them even further away. I got up, took a cigarette from the packet and gave it to her. It was long, thin, and of the menthol variety, a whiff like that of freshly brushed teeth rose up as I lit it for her.

I went over to the railing. The wall of water barely cleared it. She was just as closed off, as stubborn and resolute as before. Still, I did not want to give up. Besides, surprisingly enough, she was not actually that unpleasant to be around, no matter how difficult or aloof she pretended to be. I didn't know why, perhaps because it was impossible not to look at her in light of her husband and consider that no matter what she had managed to preserve of herself from living with him, it would be something that tended towards the positive.

"What are you planning to do?" she asked, after I had been standing a while, possibly viewing it as some sort of demonstration on my part, that I wanted to show her that I could be just as willful as her, that I was the type who would remain there right up until she spoke.

"I don't know," I said. "Have another chat with your husband, I suppose."

I regretted not having turned to see the expression on her face after I said it. From where I stood I was looking down at a courtyard between an old part and a new wing of the hospital. Several silver-colored pipes protruded from the tarmac here and there, they looked like giant worms poking their heads up. An ambulance arrived, it was met by three people in yellow raincoats.

"I'll never report him," Mrs. Gunerius said. "Regardless of what the police do, I won't report him, or testify against him, for that matter."

It took a moment for what she had just said to sink in.

"Even if I have to stand in court and lie," she added, so firmly, and with such determination that she had already responded to all appeals and attempts at persuasion that might be in the offing.

I turned around.

"I wish you would all just leave him in peace," she continued. "He has enough things to worry about."

"I'll have to talk to him all the same," I said. "We can't just overlook something like this."

I nodded, comically, it struck me afterwards, in the direction of the plaster casts on her legs. She sat with her back straight, taking short but deep drags of her toothpaste cigarette. She almost had a regal air about her now. She had managed to turn the uncomfortable position she was forced to adopt to her advantage: the impression she gave was more dignified than wretched.

"Will you be able to walk again?"

"They don't know yet," she replied.

A siren began to wail below, I heard someone shout, then a door slam shut and the squeal of tires as the vehicle took off in a hurry.

An old lady with a walking frame was approaching the door to the balcony, I walked over and opened it for her.

"Talk to Maltek instead," Mrs. Gunerius said. "It's all his fault. Everything took a turn for the worse when he came on the scene."

"Maltek?"

"Maltek. He should be easy to find."

I waited until the woman with the walker was safely across the threshold, then I left, at a quick pace, hurrying through the sound of droning voices that seemed like a perpetual feature in the green-walled corridors, irrespective of whether there were people there or not.

The villa was set back from the road with some woods behind it in an area where the rest of the houses were in very close proximity to one another. There was a front gate with cameras mounted on each pillar, but it was easy to negotiate and I didn't encounter any uniformed security or ill-tempered guard dogs on my way up the drive, which wound its way upward in an S-shape before leveling out in a flagstone-paved plateau at the top of the hill. The house was a hodgepodge of styles: part chalet, part neoclassical with its Roman columns, and part Mediterranean with its whitewashed walls. There was a high fence running atop a three-door garage, through which I could discern the top of a diving board. A black Subaru stood parked at an angle in front of the garage and I made a mental note of the number plate.

I walked up to the front door and rang the bell. Classical music could be heard from inside. I turned and looked out at the view behind me. There was nothing where the city should have been, just a huge grayish-white cloud that neither began nor ended anywhere, visibility was restricted to just a few meters beyond the wrought iron gate at the bottom of the driveway, it looked like Gunerius's property had been torn loose and launched into the void.

The door opened and the music streamed out. Gunerius was wearing a white bathrobe tied loosely around his fat body and stood leaning against the doorframe, his body at an odd angle, and judging by his blotchy face and squinting eyes he seemed heavily intoxicated. He didn't seem to recognize me. I looked at his legs, which were surprisingly thin, as though someone else's feet were sticking out, covered in gray and purple knotted veins.

"Inspector Wold," I said, in a low voice so he wouldn't quite catch it. "I have a few more questions I'd like answered."

He was drunker than I'd first thought, and was having trouble keeping his head steady, it was swaying from side to side as though trying to locate the point on his neck that could hold it up. I took advantage of his confusion to slip past him into the large foyer where a huge spiral staircase led up to the next level of the house.

The music was coming from upstairs. I started up the stairs, its enormous proportions lent something dreamlike to it.

"Hey!" Gunerius shouted from behind me.

I glanced over my shoulder as I neared the top. He still hadn't made it as far as the first step. If I was quick I could manage to check out quite a bit.

The double doors opposite were open wide, the volume of the music—an aria from a well-known opera—made everything vibrate. An assortment of bottles and drinking glasses stood upon a glass table. There were clothes in a heap on a sofa, upholstered in gold brocade with gilded tassels on the armrests. A sweet smell wafted through the room, perfume of some kind, mingled with a hint of summer and hay: cannabis, most likely. I walked over to the stereo and pulled the plug. Silence resounded, like an echo of the bustle that had just been. I was in no doubt: it was only moments since whoever had been in the room had left.

I went back out into the hall, looked left and right but spotted nobody. In the meantime, Gunerius had reached the top of the stairs. He stood in front of me out of breath, his robe having parted slightly, giving me a glimpse of his genitals, long and dark like those of a horse, before he pulled his dressing gown closed and tied the belt.

"What kind of fucking liberties do you think you can take?" he wheezed, his breathing heavy, but at the same time it was as if the exertion of climbing the stairs had siphoned off some of the drunkenness, readying him for a fight.

I heard a door closing downstairs, my first impulse was to

take the stairs but Gunerius was blocking my way. Instead I went back into the drawing room and over to the window. A man had opened a door of the Subaru and was pushing a teenage boy into the backseat. He slammed the door and glanced up at the house. Then he got into the driver's side, without any urgency, as though to let me know that he had seen me. The car reversed a little then turned and crawled down the S of the drive. The gate opened at the bottom, and it was like the car hovered for a moment before disappearing into the gray haze.

"There'll be consequences for this, I hope you realize that," Gunerius snorted. He had sat down in a chair. "Don't you all follow any rules anymore?"

I walked over to the sofa and looked through the pile of clothes, but turned up nothing other than Gunerius's own garments. A pair of tartan slippers lay on the carpet by the glass coffee table.

"What have you been smoking in here?" I asked.

Gunerius grinned. "You know as well as I do!"

"Have you supplied any underage individuals with narcotics?"

"You fuckin' bet I have! I lit one up that was sticking out of his ass, and what's more, the kid was able to take a toke through that hole!"

He pitched forward and began rummaging through the assortment of bottles.

"You would've liked it if you'd seen it," he mumbled, dropping one bottle after another onto the floor, until eventually he was left holding something that looked like egg liqueur. He began drinking right from the bottle. A streak of yellow ran from his chin and down along his neck.

"You need to learn some manners, Officer," he said. "You might be a policeman but you can't just barge in to someone's house that way. We're respectable people. We're respectable people."

He slumped as he said it, his robe opening again, revealing

two pink breasts that were squeezed flat against his swollen stomach.

"What I do is up to me and nobody else. Please try to get that into your head. And that's the difference between me and somebody like you. You can't do as you like. You have to watch yourself. You have to watch your every step."

He was barely able to articulate the words on account of all the saliva amassing in his mouth.

"You need to answer for everything you do. I don't need to answer for anything. I have other people who answer for me. You understand? That's the difference between you and me. I can get other people to do exactly as I want. I can get . . ."

It looked like he was scouring his memory for an appropriate example.

"Ha!"

He tried to make eye contact with me but his gaze drifted off.

"I could get you to do anything. I could think up anything at all, and sooner or later you'd have to do it."

He lifted his hand up into the air.

"I could get you to tidy up after me. Get you to clean up all this mess."

He looked around, trying to find something to focus his eyes upon.

"What a mess! The place is always a fucking shambles! But there's always someone who comes and cleans up after me. That's what's so nice about it. I don't need to worry. I don't need to worry about anything. Do you understand that? And do you understand what a . . ."

He took a deep breath.

"Privilege!" he practically spat out. "It is? No matter what I do, no matter how much . . ."

He filled his lungs with air again, his breasts swelled up.

" . . . crap there is, someone comes and cleans it up. While you, you can't drive five kilometers over the speed limit without answering for it. It's as simple as that."

He sneered.

"The poor, they're the only ones who think the rich are unhappy."

He gave the bottle a shake.

"That's what you buy. Freedom. And freedom, that's priceless. It's the best thing life has to offer."

My eyes were drawn to the gold tassels on the sofa. But everything in there was probably just as extravagant and expensive, even though it may not have looked it.

A poor man who wants something is a criminal, someone once said, I couldn't remember who.

Gunerius let out a heavy sigh.

"There's only one person that scares me."

He smirked.

"You probably thought no one did. But there is one. He's the only person I'm afraid of."

He looked up.

"Penniless Gunerius! He's the only one that frightens me. He's the only one that can threaten me. As for the rest of them, all I need do is this."

He tried to snap his fingers, but the result was a moist rasp.

"And they're gone."

His head swayed a little before he finally managed to fix his stare somewhere close to my face.

"You have to make out like you're doing good deeds to achieve what you want. You have to act like you're not thinking of yourself to get what you're after. That's the only capital you have, your good intentions. They're all you have to bargain with. I can skip all that. I don't need to pretend. I don't need to pass myself off as anything. I can be honest with everyone. People are so horny to do business with me that they'll go along with anything. I can tell them they're idiots and still be sure they'll do everything I ask of them. I can grab anyone's ass. I can stick my cock where I want. While you, you fool, you have to wheedle and wheedle to get yours."

He brought the bottle to his mouth, but it seemed to be empty.

"Why did you do it?" I asked.

He made a fresh attempt to make eye contact.

"Why did you assault your wife?" I asked.

For a moment it was as though a little life came into his eyes.

"Why did you beat her?"

"Fuck's sake," he slurred. "How pathetic can you be?"

"Why did you beat her?" I repeated.

He placed his hands on the armrests and tried to get up.

He slumped back into the chair and sat shaking his head.

"If I was you," he said, "if I was you, I'd fucking kill myself."

His head fell forward heavily.

The bottle suddenly slipped from his grasp.

"Christ, so disgusting," he gurgled, his eyes swimming, then he let out a large belch. I wanted to leave, but could not avert my eyes before the first jet escaped him. He threw up another three or four times, before the first bout was finished.

He remained rigid in the chair, his legs wide apart and a fan of vomit on the carpet in front.

"I'll be in touch," I said.

Before leaving I went over to the stereo, put in the plug, pressed play and turned the volume up even louder, the horns, strings, and choir made everything shake, like some divine messenger had arrived to cleanse the room unmercifully.

How many of the signs we see are only signs because we're looking for them? Anne-Sofie was like that, saw a meaning in everything, everywhere. The letters on a street sign, the ticket number in a post office line, a clock that had stopped at a certain time, the order in which traffic lights changed, which way the car ahead of us turned, everything comprised some form of message, explanation, or pointer, or the opposite: a warning, a hint about an impending disaster that could be avoided. She once got on the number 17 bus and rode it all the way to the terminus because a person who'd been sitting beside her on a bench in the park had had a book open to page 17. Black cats and ladders didn't bother her, whereas the number on our cinema seats or the row we were sitting in could cause her to cancel all her appointments the following week.

When she got sick, the signs stopped appearing to her. Or was it because she began to ignore them? She had other things on her mind, probably as simple as that. Although I hadn't cared much for the signs and had often teased her about them, there was something regrettable about the way they disappeared, I found myself missing them, willing the return of what had been so real to her, the contrivances she had used to understand the world around her, which were ditched as soon as the pains got in the way, as though it had only been a game all that time, a product of the excess energy she used to have but was no longer in possession of, something to spice up life, a luxury of sorts.

Once, when I was making fun of her for a decision she had made based on one of these signs that had appeared out of nowhere, she asked me what the difference was between what she did and what I did during my job.

Now it was like she couldn't remember any of it. It seemed like she had forgotten everything, what she used to say, what she used to do, what she liked and did not like, what she wished for and what she wanted to avoid at all costs. It was all gone, driven from her mind. As though she could no longer recall how Anne-Sofie Reichelt had been.

"Can't you stay home for a few days, now that you've put in so much overtime?" she asked. We were sitting on the sofa watching some light entertainment on the TV, a show where random members of the studio audience tried to guess how much money was contained in several burlap sacks with dollar signs on them.

"What would I do at home?"

"Be here. Keep me company."

"Keep you company while you watch TV?"

She picked up the remote control, switched off the TV, pulled her knees up to her chest, and turned to me.

"So, what do you want to talk about?" she said.

It was hard to tell whether or not she was being ironic.

"In any case, I'm right in the middle of something," I said. "You know that."

She sat mulling over what I said, I could see that. She began bumping her chin against her knees, one set of teeth coming down on the other, with a sound like clattering hooves. Then she said: "What's her name?"

No matter what I said, she would find something to seize upon.

She smiled. "That's good," she said.

"What is?"

"That at least you're done trying to pretend."

She waved her arms around in a spastic motion while mimicking my voice: "Who do you mean?"

She slapped herself on the forehead: "Who do you mean?"

Her voice grew more distorted: "Who on earth are you talking about?"

And: "Haven't got the foggiest idea!"

It was rather unsettling, she sounded like a man.

I had to make an effort to remain composed.

"It's a new case," I said, "the one I'm on at the moment."

"Okay," she said, "so what's the big deal about telling me her name?"

It was as though some of her old sharpness, shrewdness, and desire for discussion had returned, only in a hideous, twisted form.

"Inger something," I said. "But why are you so interested in her when I'm not?"

Anne-Sofie laughed.

"Inger something. That's good. Let's see. Inger, what was her name again?"

She began making faces again.

"Inger, Inger, Inger, Inger Cuntjuice, was it? Or Inger Cockbreath? Can't quite remember. But it was definitely Inger-something-or-other. Wasn't it? Wasn't it? Inger, Inger, Inger . . ."

I thought about the rolled-up newspaper pages she'd placed in my shoes the first time I was there. As if she wanted to make sure I'd come back.

"Wasn't it?" Anne-Sofie shouted, picking up a glass and throwing it at me, it hit me on the thigh and then fell to the floor, where it spun around, without smashing. I picked up my plate and went into the kitchen.

"Inger Anal!" I heard from behind me. "Was that it?" It didn't seem like she was going to drop it anytime soon, and would likely follow after me, so I hurried to the bathroom and locked the door after me. I sat down on the toilet. I could hear her moving about. And then after a while: "Kristian?"

"Kristian?"

"Where are you?"

It was a while before she tried the handle on the bathroom door.

"Hello?"

The handle went up and down furiously a few times, I heard a heavy thud against the door, then it went quiet.

"Kristian?"

I thought of Inger, what anguish had destroyed of her and what had remained, what was left and what had been lost, how she had changed and how she was still the person she had been.

"Can you open the door?"

I pictured Inger's face, could conjure it up without any problem now, could visualize all the faces she had, layer after layer of them, just as they were stored within her, all the different ones she could have, all those she'd had and all the ones she'd show me in the future.

"Can you open the door? Please, Kristian?"

I saw her shadow darkening the gap at the bottom of the door. I tried to imagine how Anne-Sofie would react if something happened to me, if I had an accident and was seriously injured, if I suddenly lay hovering between life and death, what effect the fright may have on her, whether the distress caused would bring her back to herself, if the fear of losing me would penetrate so deeply that it might manage to return some of her old self?

"Kristian?"

And I considered how everything up until now had taken place outside of me. I had been a part of what had happened, but what had happened had never become a part of me. If I was to point out one event, what would that be? If I were to relate a story to someone, which one would I choose?

"Kristian?" I heard once more, and it struck me that it could just as well be me standing outside shouting. And I thought about the old guy in the basement of number 18, how long he would end up sitting there, who would be contacted the day someone let themselves in and found him, if anybody would be at all, or if that was the very reason he was sitting there, that no one missed him, nobody noticed he was gone, there was nobody he ought to have been in touch with, no place he should have been and where the alarm would soon be raised, no place where someone might ask if someone felt like taking it upon themselves to swing by and check on Gustav, since he hadn't been seen around in a while?

"I can't remember anything from when I was small," Inger said. "Not before starting school. I don't remember anything prior to that."

I tried to think.

"Me neither," I said. "I don't even remember starting school."

"You must remember that!"

"I've probably repressed it," I said.

"You've got to be kidding."

I tried to think of something, a summer's day, an occurrence on the way to school, a squabble with my classmates, but it was like I was rummaging through the mind of another man, unfamiliar with the placement of things.

"What do you remember, then?" she asked. "Which period of your life is clearest to you?"

"This," I replied.

"This?"

"Together with you."

"Besides that?"

The wind picked up. The window catch rattled. The rain grew heavier. I turned over on my side.

"High school, maybe," I said, mostly in order to say something. "And you?"

She lay staring at the ceiling.

"Same here," she said, after pondering it for a while. "High school. Or the summer it ended. The feeling I had then. Everything open. Nothing decided. The freedom."

She told me about a friend of hers, and about a boyfriend she travelled around Europe with.

We deftly avoided broaching the subject of Halvard and

Anne-Sofie. I did not ask, she did not ask. She made no mention of him, I made no mention of her. How long could we keep them outside, pretend they didn't exist?

"It's so clear to me," she said. "That whole summer. As though everything that happened afterwards can be traced back to it. If I was to begin all over again, then that's where I'd want to start."

She turned to me and asked if I knew what she meant.

I said that I did.

"Accidents are something you bring onto yourself," Inger said. "Do you believe that's true?"

I thought about Anne-Sofie's father, a schemer and a tightwad who right up to the end had maintained that everyone was the architect of their own happiness, and who had sold off his share of the company he had run together with his older brother, without telling him, a month before it went under.

"No," I said. "I don't believe that. Do you?"

Her eyelids opened and closed slowly. I saw tears forcing their way out, pushing her eyelashes aside.

"I don't know," she said.

"Then they wouldn't be accidents," I said. "They'd be something else."

A tear pearled up in the corner of her eye, before bursting and zigzagging down her cheek.

"But you're right," she said, drying it away. "Probably best to forget."

"What do you mean?"

"Imagine if we forgot everything as soon as it was over. That'd be the best thing. If no sooner than it happened we forgot about it. Imagine we only had enough space in our memory to hold the last two or three hours. Imagine how good that would be. Imagine how happy we'd be. And if something bad happened, it would only last a couple of hours, then it would be over."

"Where would that leave us, if things were like that?" I asked.

She looked at me.

"Every time we met we'd forget about each other afterwards. Or we'd never see each other again. How would I remember to come here tomorrow, for instance?"

"Okay, twelve hours, then."

"What if I go somewhere for work and I'm away an entire day?"

"Well, okay. Twenty-four hours."

"Or just think of the families on holidays who won't know where to go the day they leave for home."

"Ach. You're so boring."

I knew she was joking but it still hurt.

"Boring?"

"Yeah. Because you think of everything."

"Is that boring?"

Her eyes were open, her gaze steady and serious, lips parted and teeth gleaming a little in the half-light.

"Yeah. You're not supposed to think of everything. No one can think of everything. You go crazy if you try to do that."

There was a shimmer in her eye, signaling the issue of another impending trickle.

"It's best to think as little as possible," she said. "The best thing is not to think at all."

She laid her head under my chin. Her body twitched, I put my arm around her and held her as tightly as I could.

"Nobody can think of everything," I said.

I noticed my body shaking in time with her shivering, reproducing the slightest movement, as though we were lying there protecting one another during a minor quake.

"Inger," I said. "Nobody can think of everything."

"I wish you could stay," she said. "I wish you never had to leave."

I wasn't sure what she meant by that.

"Sometimes when you go," she said, "I'm left in doubt as to whether you've actually been here. If you were here just moments ago. Or if it's been ages. If it's been days since."

I thought about something I'd heard once, about how you had to stay a certain amount of time in any particular place before the soul could settle, that you had to be there awhile before you had really been there. And I thought about how Inger's apartment had yet to become such a place, that there was still nothing left in my wake when I departed.

I was awoken by her arm coming down on my face. I lifted it off. She was asleep. Her mouth lay open, as though she wasn't getting enough air. I looked at her face. I thought about the photographs I had seen of Maria and tried looking for a resemblance. But there was something unpleasant about studying her that way, so closely, without her being aware of it, like observing a picture that could come to life at any moment. Her lips suddenly began to tighten. It looked like she was trying to say something.

Then I must have fallen back asleep, because when I opened my eyes again, Inger was dressed and seated beside me.

"Come on," she said. "I want to show you something."

She pulled me up out of bed, confusedly I began to gather up my clothes.

She waited until I was dressed. Then she took my hand.

"Come on," she said.

The TV was on in the living room, a freeze-frame quivering on the screen, a still picture of some figures in white, surrounded by garish, shuddering colors.

Inger led me to the sofa. We sat down, she pressed a button on the remote control and the figures came to life: girls in white outfits and belts in different colors jumping around on a blue mat, they looked like sparrows until they began kicking and swinging at one another with loud cries.

The picture zoomed in on one of them.

"That's Maria," Inger said.

The camera tried to keep her in frame, but she moved around so much that there were really only a few glimpses of her now and then, and her hair was constantly dancing in front of her face. After a while the camera zoomed out again. Calm descended upon the leaping gathering.

"How old is she there?" I asked.

"Eleven."

The spectacle finished, the white-clothed figures bowed to one another, then there was an abrupt cut to a close-up of Maria, standing drinking from a bottle by a straw. The person filming moved even closer, without any visible reaction from Maria to indicate whether or not she minded.

"Happy with the result?" a man asked.

His voice resounded in the room, in such proximity as he must have been to the microphone on the camera.

Maria merely rolled her eyes.

"Tired?" the man asked.

I recognized the voice.

"No," she replied, without her lips letting go of the straw.

"Do you think you'll make the belt?" her father asked.

Maria stared fixedly at the lens without answering. Then there was a gurgling sound. She looked down. The straw disappeared from the picture.

"Dunno," she said.

"Will you be very disappointed if you don't get it?" Halvard asked.

A shudder passed through me: it was like he was in the room with us, as though he were the one sitting here showing me the film. The three of them, I thought, now they're together again. Now the family is gathered around.

Then he repeated the question, which his daughter had neglected to answer. His voice thundered. I got it into my head that it was me he was speaking to. He was saying: This world is mine, Maria's, and Inger's. You have no place here.

Maria leaned forward, stuck her tongue into the camera and pulled a horrible face.

Inger paused the picture with the remote control. Then she

pressed another button and the video began going backwards, movement by jerking movement.

Maria's grimace closed like a bag being tied up.

"There," Inger said, stopping the film. "That's my Maria."

I looked at the face on the screen. Her eyes gleamed as they stared out of the TV, right at me, something approaching surprise in them, it seemed, at the sight of someone she hadn't seen in the living room before. She had a brazen expression about her mouth, an indeterminate look, somewhere between pout and grimace. Inger put down the remote control, leaving the picture frozen.

At first I was unsure what to do, whether I should say something or ask what she had meant. But after looking at the enlarged face of the girl for a while, it was as though I could see it too, see her the way she had been.

And what I saw was someone I did not like. An unpleasant person. A spoiled child. Cheeky and unruly, demanding, never satisfied, never content with anything, aggrieved by the slightest thing. I saw it in her expression. Inger had done everything for her and still it hadn't been enough. She had the look on her face of somebody whose default mood was one of dissatisfaction, someone dissatisfied with everything presented to her, a dissatisfaction that took up all the space and made it impossible for her to think about anyone other than herself.

She had something repugnant about her. So sure that the world existed solely for her and so displeased with everything it had to offer. No matter what her mother did for her, she was met with a surly response. The more she was at her beck and call, the more she was treated with disrespect. The more care and consideration the abhorrent child was shown, the more calculated her abuse became.

I could not stand her.

It was only right for Inger to give her a telling off that night, it was no less than she deserved.

And I pictured her abused, battered body and I thought that if there was one thing that wasn't terrible, it was what had happened to her.

I glanced at Inger. She was mesmerized, couldn't take her eyes from the screen, a glow reflected on her cheeks.

She saw her Maria.

But it was a girl who didn't exist, who never had, other than as her Maria, the way she was in her eyes, the daughter she wished she would be, hoped she would become, but not how she was.

I looked back at the screen. The longer the picture remained, the greater the difference was between the girl Inger had told me about and the person I now understood had lived with her. The Maria you remember has never lived, I thought. The Maria you miss will never be found, because she does not exist. The Maria you bury one day will not be, and was not, the person you thought she was.

And I felt a sudden relief, like a threat had been lifted, like something I had been afraid was going to come and ruin things for us had turned out to be something we need not fear after all.

I stood looking at the books on Inger's shelves, all kinds, new and old, placed there without any semblance of a system, or with one that was incomprehensible to everyone but her. I recognized a spine here and there: I had a small feeling of satisfaction each time, as if there lay some sort of affirmation in it.

"Is it still raining?" she asked.

"Yes. It never lets up."

"Is there anybody out at all?"

It was as if she were interrogating me about a life outside that she no longer participated in. Inside, in the warm, yellow living room, we were in our own world. But I was the only one of us who had an additional existence.

I went to get the plastic bag with the wine I had purchased on the way, two bottles from the shelf nearest the till.

"Isn't it inconvenient, being without a car when you have to be out and about talking to people?" she asked.

I uncorked the bottle carefully and poured us both a glass before sitting down on the sofa, we sat at each end, our legs entwined.

"The advantage is I can drink whenever I want," I said, wishing we could sit like that chatting about trivial things all day long.

"Why don't you take a taxi?"

"I don't know."

She could see I was pondering something and asked what it was.

I took a gulp of wine.

"Just something my father said to me once."

"Which was?"

"Never take a cab."

"Was that it?"

"That was it. Never take a cab."

Inger smiled. "Is that the reason?"

"Maybe."

"Are you alike?"

"In appearance?"

"In any way."

I considered it for a moment, tried to collect my thoughts. There was something fraudulent, I felt, about passing comment on oneself, like being questioned about someone I didn't know. It struck me that no matter what I said it would be pure conjecture.

"He died when I was fifteen."

Inger held the glass in her hand, had not yet brought it to her lips. She was waiting for me to continue.

"There are times," I said, "when I think it made it easier for me. To be like him, I mean. We were actually very different. Became more and more so as time went on. But then he died. And I don't know, but I've often thought that if he hadn't passed away then maybe I would have continued, carried on with what I'd started, which was to be as unlike him as possible. As opposed to how things are, now that he isn't around. As though I'd taken his place after he'd vacated it."

I looked at Inger, unsure if any of what I had said made sense.

"That the way marked out for me was actually supposed to be the opposite of his. But all of a sudden his path lay open and I ended up taking that instead."

"How come you haven't had any children yourself?"

"Dunno." I couldn't face thinking about it. "It's just turned out like that."

A grotesque thought occurred to me: *we're both childless.*

Fortunately she didn't pursue the subject.

"Who's your best friend?" she asked.

I had to laugh.

"Why are you laughing?"

"Because," I said, without being aware of what gave rise to it myself.

"Because?"

"Because I don't have a clue how to answer that!" I said.

"Don't you have any friends?" she asked, surprised.

"Not that I know of!" I laughed.

"No one at work?"

Inger was quite solemn.

"It would have to be Bernhard, I suppose."

"Bernhard?"

"Yeah."

"Why is he your best friend?"

"Because," I said. There was something annoying, but at the same time gratifying, about her unwillingness to give in, about the fact that she kept on quizzing me.

"Because?"

"Because we . . ."

I stopped up, but simultaneously realized that the time was right, that if I was ever going to tell anybody, then it was her, at this moment.

"Something happened," I said, "when we were in Krakow last year."

"You and him?"

"Bernhard, yes."

I took my time, not out of reluctance, but because I was searching for the right words, I had never imagined I would tell the story to anyone, and correspondingly had never given any thought as to how it ought to be presented.

"We were in Krakow in connection with a case. A whole busload of people had died. There were some Norwegians involved, and Bernhard and I had been assigned to follow the trail from here to Poland."

Inger had been curled up at her end of the sofa, now she stretched out her legs, her feet touching my side.

"The whole investigation was hopeless. The newspapers wrote that we'd helped clear it up. The truth was that it was never solved. A few people way down the food chain were convicted, the rest walked."

Inger didn't say anything, just listened, gave me the time I needed.

"And while we were there, we came across this guy, a pimp, who, well, it doesn't matter, he didn't have any direct connection to our case but he kept cropping up in relation to all manner of things, we were running into him or encountering his name the whole time, he was the kind who had a finger in every pie, and was never charged with anything, who made sure any involvement he had could never be traced back to him."

Despite my resolving to tell her, I felt a sudden anxiety about continuing. I drained my glass. Inger sat just as calmly and attentively. Her indulgence was almost frightening. I could not help but think it was more than I deserved.

"Bernhard, in particular," I said, without quite knowing why, "let it get to him, everything about this guy, who was, pretty much, the worst of a very bad lot, and who we realized would continue to always get away scot-free. We met one of his girls, and among other things . . ."

I could see by Inger's face that she'd rather not know.

"Anyway," I said, "the night before we were due to leave, we were at one of the bars he owned. We'd had quite a lot to drink. And at some stage during the evening Bernhard went to the toilet, but then he suddenly returned, a wild look in his eyes, and dragged me, without explanation, towards the toilets, which were in the backyard, in a kind of passageway, and past them into a lean-to with a few trash cans beneath. In there, propped up against one of them, stood the pimp, so drunk he could hardly stand. And I don't know how, but all of a sudden Bernhard was holding a length of pipe in his hand, and before I knew it he was laying into him with it. The pimp just went down, not a sound escaped him. And Bernhard just kept on hitting him. Then he handed me the pipe. I can't remember what was going through my mind exactly. That we had to get out of there, I think. But then suddenly I was standing there beating away at him as well."

She wasn't looking at me anymore, as though what she'd heard had been enough.

"Bernhard egged me on with each blow," I said. "The figure on the ground bore less and less resemblance to a man. I don't know how long we kept it up. Then we left, quite calmly, side-by-side. We brought the pipe with us and waited until we reached a bridge a fair distance away before getting rid of it."

I regretted saying the last part, and feared that it might put an end to her indulgence.

"We flew home the next day. Bernhard hasn't mentioned a word about it since. Neither have I. Not to him, not to anyone."

"So that," I smiled, "is why Bernhard is my best friend. Aren't they the best friends, the ones you share secrets with?"

Inger didn't answer.

I stroked her foot.

"It's only Bernhard and you I have secrets with."

Inger didn't say anything, but I could tell she was thinking about what had happened, and considered it as something that had turned out the way it had turned out, not as something that should not have occurred or ought to have been carried out differently. She did not accept what I had done, but she accepted me, the person who had done it.

I looked at her again. Maria was not in her thoughts now. For the time being she had forgotten she had a daughter. Right then and there she was alone, with me. The two of us were alone together. For the moment none of the other stuff reached us.

"A lot of the time," she said, after a long while, "the things we do aren't the same as what we intended."

She had taken my side. She would have taken my side no matter what I told her.

But the warm glow enveloping us where we sat, just the two

of us, also gave rise to anxiety, of a type I had not felt before, as if it were only a matter of time before the warmth dissipated, as if it had its allotted time and that every minute we sat there, letting ourselves be surrounded by it, used up what remained.

I wanted to jump up and run out of the house, save as much of it as possible until the next time we met.

And I wanted to be there, to stay put, and remain seated until time ran through our fingers, only to linger a while longer, then a while longer, and longer after that.

"So many things turn out differently than planned," she said. "But maybe that's the way it has to be?"

She had a slightly absentminded look.

"I used to . . ." she said, still distant.

Those words, I thought, *used to*: they had, and would continue to have, gruesome significance for her.

"I used to always go around believing that the way things were, how I and everything around me was, that it was all temporary. As though I was walking around just waiting for something to happen, something that would change it all, make things take a turn, and then, from that day on, everything would be as it should, the way it was supposed to be from the start, but that it just hadn't taken place yet. I was certain of it, I thought about it every single day, that if I was just patient, then one sunny day . . . Over time it was like the thought never really left me. Do you know what I mean? It was always there, the thought that this wasn't how it was meant to be, that things should have actually been completely different. Always thinking about how things could have been otherwise, and could have been better, and how those circumstances would be more befitting, more in line with what I wanted, what I felt like, what suited me, and what I had an aptitude for. As though I was always being cheated of the occasion I needed to bring out the best in myself, as though the opportunity to prove my worth was constantly withheld from me. I waited and waited. Quite certain that things would only be the way they were for a limited time. Do you understand? As if there was always a thought standing between me and what I did, a thought preventing me from doing it wholeheartedly. A thought that stood between me and the people I knew, as well as the people I was with. Because I went around waiting for the day when I would be myself. As though there were a string within me that had yet to be plucked. A sound that nobody had yet heard."

"That sound . . ." I started to say.

But before I could go on, she leaned over, ran her hand over the side of my head and cheek and said: "You're kind."

I thought: Now you're yourself, when you're not thinking about what's happened.

"But it's not possible to think like that anymore," she said, and looked at me and smiled. Suddenly, as though something had pierced her eye, a single tear ran down her cheek. But there was no discernible change in her expression, she continued to smile, as if they came from two different places within her, the smile and the tear. Part of her remembered, and another part managed to avoid it.

But where did the pain go in the minutes and seconds she forgot it?

A large cloud drifted by in the window behind her, the room grew darker, the day had bounded off. I did not want to leave. I did not want to find Maria. I wanted to be together with Inger. I wanted to preserve what we had, keep it going, exactly how it was now. With a horrible feeling, I glanced at my watch.

We looked at each other for a while.

I got to my feet. Inger followed me to the door, brushed her hand against mine as we walked through the hall but did not take hold of it. I wanted to take her with me, back into the bedroom, into the darkness, where nothing else existed.

We kissed.

"Don't take a taxi," she said.

I gave the license plate number I had noted at Gunerius's to Bernhard, without holding out much hope of it leading to anything. While we were waiting, I asked Bernhard if the name Maltek meant anything to him. He chewed on it, then shook his head.

"Sounds shady," he said.

The digits descended over the screen like an avalanche, like the rain that had been teeming down for four or five weeks now, speculation was rife, environmentalists blamed heavy industry, industry blamed the authorities while they, or a couple of ministers at least, had intimated that terrorists were behind it.

"You know Kaczorowski," I said.

I tried to remember what he looked like, the Polish pimp, but all I could picture was that trademark white jacket of his, which was black when we left him.

"Haven't heard of him either," Bernhard said, without turning around.

I had looked up his name a few times, but it had not appeared anywhere, not in any police records, newspapers, or on the Net. It was like he had disappeared without a trace, or no one had ever found him, he was still lying there, mutilated, between the trash cans in the alley.

"Actually," Bernhard said, and leaned closer to the screen. "If it's a Jarosz Maltek you mean, then I do know who he is. He's the guy who owns a black Subaru Legacy 2.0R," he said, tipping back in his chair.

I looked at the line he was pointing out to me.

"Easy as that," he said. "But nothing about him on file, as far as I can see."

"I know," I said. "His address will do."

"A paragon of virtue," I added, as I saw the inquisitive look on Bernhard's face as he handed me the printout.

Risberg called out to me as I was standing at the coffee machine. His tone of voice wasn't encouraging. I brought the scorching hot paper cup with me into his office, which had floor-to-ceiling windows facing the rest of the open plan floor, Risberg having requested them himself during recent renovations, with the stated intention of being more "visible" and "approachable" as boss.

He motioned for me to sit.

I suddenly remembered something he'd said back when he interviewed me for his section. "An investigator shouldn't be too good. An investigator shouldn't tax his intellect too much. Most cases have an awfully simple explanation. The way things initially appear are the way they are. Criminals are stupid, they leave such an obvious trail behind them that it can be hard to take them seriously." And I recalled a case, one of my first, where the amount of evidence implicating the suspect was so overwhelming that for a long time I thought it had been planted in order to point in the direction of his guilt.

"How's it going?" Risberg asked.

"With what?"

I tried to take a sip of my coffee but it burned the tip of my tongue.

Risberg gave a grunt of indignation.

"Listen, I asked you to take a look into this business with Mrs. Gunerius, not mount a crusade against the wealthiest man in the city!"

"Crusade?"

"I received a call from the commissioner. You understand? The commissioner. Gunerius's lawyer called and took it up with her directly, not me, get it? And then I get a call from her, enquiring as to what the hell we're up to."

"I've got a lead."

"A lead? Gunerius says it was an accident, Mrs. Gunerius says it was an accident, so how can you have a lead?"

"There's something going on. And it was no accident, his wife has already said as much."

I was about to tell him about Gunerius but thought better of it, something told me it would be wise to keep it to myself for the time being.

Instead I said: "She's given me a name to check out."

Risberg groaned. "What is with you at the moment?"

"What do you mean?"

He threw his hands up in a gesture of exasperation. "First the missing person case, which you were supposed to make sure was wound up in a proper manner, but from what I hear seems more like it's been reopened . . . ?"

He paused for a moment, as though to let me know that if I wanted I could choose to interpret that as a question.

And when I didn't reply: "And then all this with Gunerius, where you've found out everything you need to know yet continue to dig, continue to provoke; according to the commissioner, Gunerius is starting to wonder if there's something personal about this on your part. And his lawyer says you were downright offensive the last time you paid him a visit."

"So, what you're telling me is to desist in going any further with what I've got?"

Risberg writhed in his chair, as if the whole situation caused an allergic reaction.

"By the way, I could do with a search warrant," I said.

Risberg rolled his eyes. "For?"

"Gunerius," I said. "For their home address."

Risberg closed his eyes and brushed his hair back from his forehead a few times in quick succession.

"The point is that if you persist in this manner, then we could be looking at a harassment suit. The lawyer was crystal clear about that."

"So you mean," I said, "that the risk of that is sufficient reason to cease all further investigation."

The formal wording had the desired effect: Risberg was peeved and frustrated.

"All I'm saying," he began, but he stopped, he caught sight of something or other that left him tongue-tied.

Then he turned back to me, anxious, it seemed, that I might see it too. I looked out. Bernhard was approaching with his arm around somebody, a woman, drenched to the skin, with her hair stuck to her face. It was Inger. I got to my feet.

"Wold," Risberg said, having recognized her. "What the hell is going on?"

I put the coffee down on his desk and hurried out. Inger looked dead on her feet but smiled when she saw me. I went over to them, signaled to Bernhard that I could take it from here, he gave me a look as I put my arm around Inger and led her in the direction of my office. Her clothes were soaking wet, she seemed distraught and her teeth were chattering from the cold. I was aware of Risberg standing in his doorway watching us.

She shivered when we entered my office.

"Get out of those wet things," I said. "Stay here, I'll go and find something you can dry off with."

I helped her off with her coat, then went out to the changing room and found a towel. I met Bernhard on the way back but raised my hand to cut him short before he had a chance to say anything.

Inger was getting undressed. I dried her hair with the towel and patted her face with it.

"Is there anything wrong?" I asked. "Has something happened?"

She shook her head.

"I just had to see you," she said. "I can't stand being there on my own."

She began to cry. I helped her as she continued to undress,

her clothes lying in wet clumps all over the floor. I dried her off and rubbed her briskly to warm her up. We stood there afterwards and held one another. She pulled my shirt up from my trousers, and ran her hands, which were cold but soon grew warm, over my back.

"Kristian," she said.

I bent down, met her lips, and allowed a wonderful reeling sensation to take hold. A few moments later, my trousers were off, Inger was sitting on the desk facing me, our mouths still joined as she opened her legs and let me inside her. None of the sounds I uttered were released, they remained within her, she consumed them, and when she groaned I felt it like a tremor in the cavity of my mouth, a jolt down my throat, we were in one another, stuck fast, such that everything remained within us, nothing was released, nothing was lost.

A shop stocking films, magazines, and various sex toys was situated on the ground floor of Malek's address. It occurred to me that I might have been there before in connection with a case, but I wasn't sure. A young man with a childish face and the body of heavyweight boxer manned the register. I approached him. He had an overripe pimple on the wing of his nose.

I asked for Malek. He shook his head. I showed him my badge and asked again.

"Just a moment," he said, his voice was gruff, lending yet another possible age to those imaginable, and he disappeared behind a door covered with a curtain.

I ran my eye over the premises. There were rows and rows of DVDs, arranged alphabetically by title, from what I could see. *Bad Boy, Benny's Heaven, Billy the Kid*. One of the covers featured a teenage boy in the process of swallowing the whole of an old man's sexual appendage: the old guy's testicles were protruding from his gaping mouth like a tumor. Four or five people wandered slowly between the shelves, pausing, then moving on, then stopping again, as though they had a clear picture in their minds of what they wanted but had so far searched in vain. There was a mannequin by the counter dressed in an army hat with a dildo attached to a belt around its waist, the rubber member pointed directly at me.

The heavyweight reemerged.

"You're to wait here," he said, then returned to his position behind the counter and surveyed the premises, as though I had already left.

The door chime sounded. A heavyset man entered. The guy behind the counter must have given him a sign, because he came right over and shook my hand. He uttered a name I did not manage to catch, but it was not Malek. He asked me to accompany him. We went out into the street, in a door to the left of the shop, through to an enclosed yard, and into an old outbuilding, which had been converted and now housed a not-inelegant office with large windows and partial glass roofing.

The meathead grabbed my arm.

"Watch what you say," he mumbled.

"What?"

He nodded in the direction of the glass-cube office at the top of a set of stairs.

"He's in a bad mood."

"Maltek, you mean?"

"And he's dangerous when he's in a bad mood. He can just explode," he said, seeming scared, as though warning himself and not me.

He said something else as he started up the steps, but the sound of the rain drowned it out.

I looked around as we went up the staircase, the windows of the buildings surrounding the yard were small with matching curtains, a man in a white undershirt stood smoking behind one window that was open slightly, in another I glimpsed the face of a young girl, for a moment I thought it was Maria, not because she bore any resemblance, but because I wanted it to be.

I was shown into a large office on the second floor. The rain thrumming on the glass roof made a pleasant sound, a soft thudding that almost formed a continuous hum. A man, the same one I had seen pushing the boy into the black Subaru, was sitting behind a desk wrapping up a telephone call. My escort sat down on a chair. The man got to his feet and presented himself as Maltek. He had a large ring that hurt my hand as he shook it. He then smiled, apologized, and displayed the ring to me, which had an inset metal swastika. He asked if I would like a drink, which I declined, then he offered me a chair and I sat down.

"Some weather we're having!"

He sounded like a girl when he spoke, on the verge of giggling.

I nodded towards the enclosed yard, of which the glass window behind the chair occupied by his bodyguard, if that was what he was, allowed an ample view.

"Do you run a hotel as well?" I asked.

"Yes," Maltek said, tittering.

"And a brothel?"

"Oh, no," he said, feigning offense at the assumption. "After all, that's against the law!"

He glanced at the bodyguard.

"You should know that, being a policeman and all!"

He stifled a small fit of laughter. I could not make up my mind about the gurgling, girlish chuckling, whether it was due to him being particularly worked up at that particular moment, or if it was just how he usually was. I was inclined to believe the latter.

"The ring," I said. "Why do you wear it?"

He looked at it, then made a fist and punched the air in my direction.

"Are you a Nazi?"

"Yes," he said. "Aren't you?"

He suppressed a fresh outburst of laughter, a snorting escaped his nose and it didn't appear as if he was going to be able to contain himself much longer. Then he assumed a serious tone.

"You can say what you like about Hitler. He made a lot of mistakes, I'm well aware of that. But how he handled the Jews. Jesus! You can't take that away from him!"

He shot me an innocent look.

Then he changed, became serious. "I'm only kidding, of course. I mean, what happened to them was terrible! Really terrible!"

He smiled: "But having a different opinion, that's not against the law now, is it?"

He picked up a hand-rolled cigarette from the desk.

"Just like this isn't illegal either."

He lit it and took a deep drag. It was the same smell as had pervaded Gunerius's drawing room.

"Illegal to sell but not to use. Just like I can be a Nazi in theory, but not in practice. Just like anyone is free to sell their body to whomever they want, as long as it doesn't take place in a brothel."

He laughed, then held the joint out to me. I shook my head. The odor was nauseous. I took out my cigarettes. Maltek put it between his lips and leaned back with his hands behind his head.

"You've got some strange laws in this country."

Only the slightest deviation in his tone of voice, that was the only hint there was of an accent.

"Makes you want to get involved in the rough-and-tumble of politics yourself at times. Bring a little order to the chaos."

I lit up a cigarette, the initial drag made me dizzy, I couldn't remember the last time I had eaten.

"But no matter how strange they are, I've learned them well. I've studied your laws very closely. I know exactly where the line goes. And, of course, I make sure to keep on the right side of it."

He flung his arms wide.

"What's the point in illegality when you can get away with most things within the law?"

Every time he finished a sentence he shot a glance at his employee, whom I couldn't see from where I was sitting, as though he needed acknowledgement of what he had said before embarking on a new bout of eunuch-like laughter.

"And operating outside the law, that's something you never do?" I asked.

He sat for a time, smoking and looking pensive.

"You know, when it comes down to it, we're all Jews really," he said.

He blew some rings of smoke that trembled on the air, putting me in mind of athletics.

"Wouldn't you agree? What was it he said again, that old foreign minister of yours? We are all Serbs. And he was right. We are all Serbs, we're all Jews. Ha ha! We're all equally rotten!"

"No pimping?" I asked, without holding out any great hope of steering the conversation towards another subject.

"Do you know what the difference between butter and margarine is, by the way?" he asked. "Butter is made from cow's milk, margarine is made from fat. Animal fat. That's why we still view real butter as having some sort of status. A few years ago, a man in Germany murdered his wife because she could only afford to buy margarine. When they asked him why, he said: We lost all our money and hadn't enough to buy butter, and my wife said she wanted to die so I killed her. Simple as that. A mercy killing, wouldn't you say, Inspector?"

"No pimping?" I repeated.

"Hitler was a vegetarian of course, a very strict one, but he did eat margarine. He even lauded a Jewish scientist who researched alternative methods of producing margarine. It's true. The scientist ran a factory in the Ruhr where they made soap from coal and experimented with synthesizing margarine from the same source. Ordinarily he would of course have been sent off to a concentration camp, but instead he received funding from the Nazis and did actually manage to manufacture a passable margarine based on coal. Hitler and Göring were both wildly enthusiastic and decreed that the margarine maker and his family were to be considered honorary Aryans. Yes, he was even decorated with two of Germany's highest military awards for his service. His company still exists today, Imhausen, you've probably heard of it. They were the ones who sold chemicals to Libya during the sanctions in the 1980s, if you recall?

"Besides, it's still the same," Maltek said, without waiting for a response, "when you're in my line of business, you're all the more dependent on keeping things in order, staying on the straight and narrow, you'd know what I mean better than most, simply because you have to reckon with being checked out every once in a while. Keep all your accounts in perfect order, in case of any clampdown. I've been at it for a few years now, and let me tell you, I've never had so much as one single comment in the margins of my books. Ever!"

He banged the desk.

"While county governors and public accountants, they're free to engage in all kinds of crooked business before anyone hits upon the crazy idea of investigating them. You get my point? I've got to think it through carefully every time I give someone a hug, while the priest, he can feel up whomever he wants. Rather unfair, wouldn't you agree? But that's the way it is. That's just the way it is."

He let out a heavy sigh.

"The law is like the weather," he said, and tittered. "Everyone thinks it's a pain in the ass but no one does anything about it."

His deranged cheerfulness annoyed me, but my irritation waned as time passed and I grew more and more convinced that he would carry on that way no matter who was sitting across the desk from him, and besides, the tobacco tasted good, in addition to keeping the cloying, nauseous aroma of the marijuana at bay.

"Tell me, Inspector, if all you had to do was press a button to kill a wealthy man in China and inherit all his money, would you do it?"

He sat there with his mouth wide open.

"Would you?" I asked.

He splayed his fingers across his chest and pulled a peculiar face, he looked like a footballer who had just been shown a yellow card, and it was only then I noticed the nail polish on his fingers, alternating between red and black.

"Me?" he said. "Why, I'm a philanthropist! And proud of it!" he cried, becoming more theatrical the longer he spoke, his facial expressions shifting with greater frequency, as though he had a certain number at his disposal and had set a target of presenting each one.

"I love people, Inspector. I love everyone. There's nobody I condemn. Even the ones who've done me wrong, I love. I bear no grudges. You can be sure of that, Inspector. Even people who speak ill of me, I love. They do it because they don't know any better. You won't hear a bad word from me about anyone."

It was impossible to determine whether he was utterly convinced of what he was saying or whether he was being sarcastic in the extreme.

"Forgiveness," he said, "look, that's the easiest thing in the world. And love is what drives us all."

I tried to think up some way of interrupting his sermon, but I ended up just sitting and listening.

"If I hadn't wound up here," Maltek said, "I would have been a priest. And I would have opened up the church to all. Transformed it into the temple of love it's supposed to be. Let in all those who are turned away elsewhere. Let all the children come unto me, not only the ones who've behaved themselves. Those too of course, but the others as well. The whole caboodle. And I'd tell them it makes no difference what they're like or what they've done because that's the way God made man. Everything we do, we do because God placed that possibility within us when he created us."

He dispensed with the bombast.

"I mean, what's the point of God if he doesn't like pedophiles?"

He gave me a look of genuine bewilderment and indignation.

"So in my church," he said, "there'd be space for you too, Inspector, no matter what kind of depravities may appear on your record."

He began to cough, but all the same I did not take the opportunity to speak.

"What do we need more?" he said. "Water or diamonds?"

There was no stopping him now, he had no time to wait for an answer, as if his mind was moving at such speed that the pace of those around him appeared unbearably slow.

"But which is more expensive? You get me? It's meaningless, all of it. The North American Indians had something they called potlatch, where they gave gifts in order to humiliate one another. One chief would present another chief with two buffalo hides. Then the recipient would have to give something better in return. The whole point was to outdo one another. Every present required further reciprocation, an acknowledgement by way of something even bigger and better. Two hides would become eight hides. Eight hides would become two horses. Two horses would become two horses and a squaw. And thus it continued. You see the problem with that, right? How do you end once you've started? After all, the one who stopped would be the loser. Sometimes they got really carried away. They'd kill their own braves and deliver them to the other tribe. Ha ha! What do you say to that?"

I reflected on how useless all this knowledge of his was.

"That's something you can mull over, Inspector. How do you put an end to a potlatch?"

I heard the bodyguard's voice from behind and felt momentarily threatened, even after I understood that he was just on the phone.

"We all act in our own best interests, every single one of us. That goes for whatever line of business you're in, smut or charity, it makes no difference. That's how it works. We help one another best by looking after number one. My customers only think of themselves, and I only think of myself, and yet both sides are satisfied. Strange, perhaps, but that's how it is. The helping hand is most effective when it's invisible."

"So, what is it you help people with?" I asked. "What is it you actually do, apart from sell magazines and run a hotel?"

"What I do?" he whispered, letting out a cackle before turning serious.

"Listen, I could sit here jabbering away all day, as I'm sure you could. But duty calls. I have a very large consignment of blow down in the basement," he laughed, "soon to be cut."

Yet another glance towards the brute in the corner.

"What is the nature of your relationship with Frederik Gunerius?" I asked.

Maltek shrugged.

"He's a client. A reliable client. I sell, he buys."

"What does he buy?"

Maltek smiled. "Nothing illegal. But then again not something he'd like me standing in the town square shouting about through a megaphone."

"You can choose, either here or down at the station, it's up to you."

His smile dissolved with a sniffle, his nose filled with mucus and he sounded like he had a cold when he said: "You've been in the shop, haven't you? You've seen what I stock. So then you have a fair idea of what Gunerius likes."

"And that's it?"

He nodded, took one last greedy drag of the joint and stubbed it out.

"What about boys?"

"What about them?"

"You had a boy with you, the last time you were there. Why?"

Maltek gave a puzzled look, not at me, but at his bodyguard.

"You were there two days ago," I continued. "And there was an underage boy with you both. Who was he? And what was he doing there?"

"In your dreams," Maltek said, without any noticeable expression either of surprise or a desire to conceal something, other than the fact that the laughter had released its hold upon him for the time being.

"How usual is it for you to go to your customers' houses and deliver goods personally?"

"Highly unusual," Maltek said, and smiled. "So much so in fact, I'd have to say I've never done it. Yes, because it's a criminal offence to volunteer false information when being interviewed by the police, isn't it?

"By the way," he said and winked to his employee, "do you know what the Holocaust was to Hitler?"

"What about Mrs. Gunerius?" I said. "What kind of differences have the two of you had?"

"Listen," Maltek said, "that stuff Gunerius wanks off to at night might well be some real filth. Even *I* might be of that view. But it's no worse than a lot of the other stuff I sell. And that's about all there is to it."

He'd regained his jaunty demeanor and returned to exchanging knowing glances with his bodyguard.

"When do you think a man is at his most selfish?" he asked. "I'd say it's in the last moments, the last thirty seconds or so before he comes."

He raised a finger.

"And when does a woman derive her greatest pleasure from a man? That's right. In the last moments, the last half-minute or so before he comes. You see?"

Once again my thoughts drifted to the pimp in Krakow, as though only now, over a year later, he had risen from the grave and begun to haunt me. Had the police found him and viewed it as only fair and proper, how he had met his end, that what had happened was best for everyone involved, and left it at that? Or had a few of his cronies cleared up the mess on the quiet and then set out themselves in full cry after the killers, scouring the streets of Krakow, in a hunt that still proved fruitless? Or maybe they were happy too? Maybe everyone saw it the same way, that the world was rid of a problem? Maybe nobody on either side of the law had any interest in finding out who was responsible for how Kaczorowski met his brutal end?

"Envy," Maltek said. "A factor you have to take into consideration, and one that's hard to overestimate. I'm all too well aware of it. They begrudge me what I have, some people. It gets to them when they hear how well I'm doing. I can see how their fingers itch when they come here. All they want to do is pick up a stone and smash my lovely roof."

I thought of the senseless joy I had felt as I battered the pimp, the utter delight it had been to take his life, the rush I had experienced as I stood with the pipe in my hands knowing it was up to me to decide whether the scumbag would live or die.

Was it the same delight Maltek felt when somebody cringed beneath him, when, beside themselves with fear for what he might subject them to, they gave him everything he wanted, admitted whatever he wanted to hear or betrayed whomever it might be he was after?

"But that's the price you pay for success," he said. "I'm making money hand over fist, you do know that? It's like there's no end to it. A lot of the stock I take in is gone within two or three days. It sells itself. You know? I don't need to lift a finger. No marketing, nothing. Pornography is like a machine that keeps on going and going, a perpetual motion machine that needs no fuel, no maintenance, nothing at all."

I couldn't resist the temptation to glance upwards. The roof looked like it was coated in a viscous, transparent pulp covered in dots moving around at a terrible speed.

"Should adders be convicted for poisoning?" Maltek said. "Or spiders for attempted strangulation. What's your opinion? You must have given some thought to that?"

"If we took a look around your hotel," I said, "what would we find?"

Maltek shrugged and kept his shoulders raised.

"Well, it's not The Grand," he said. "But the clientele are good sorts. Some of them have their eccentricities. Then again, who doesn't? To each their own, some like the mother and some like the daughter, isn't that what they say? I can't exactly ask them for character references, now can I? When all they want is a shower and a bed for the night?"

His mouth moved incessantly, as though a certain amount of words had to be expelled before he could allow it to rest.

"What with this weather we're having as well," he said. "Is it ever going to end? What do you think, Inspector? Is it climate change? Are we in danger of destroying Mother Earth? Or is the whole debate merely our new, evolved manner of chatting about the weather?"

I turned off my phone before hanging up my jacket. I'd read about that in the paper: one of the ten telltale signs of infidelity. Anne-Sofie was wearing the blue dress with white polka dots, I couldn't remember the last time I'd seen her in it, I associated it with summer. She didn't say anything but seemed in a better mood, and had dinner ready when I arrived. The sausages were overcooked and the mashed potato was full of floury lumps, but that didn't matter, the important thing was that she had made it, that the table was set and the saucepans were ready to be placed on the cork trivets that were already out.

I began to eat. I was aware of her following me with her eyes. "Good?" she asked after a while.

I looked up and nodded. Her hand was resting on the table, right by my plate. She smiled. I smiled back. Then I put down my knife and fork, placed my hand on top of hers, which was cold and moist to the touch, as if she only had the slightest warmth left in her, not enough to reach her extremities: it felt similar to the hand of someone just deceased that I'd once held, cool and clammy at the same time.

I continued eating. She just sat there picking at her food, but there was even something affected about the way she did that. Yes, she was taking pains to try and express something or other, without me being able to quite understand how I was supposed to interpret it.

"What have you done today?" she asked, with the stress on "you" as if she wanted to remind me that she also had a day's work behind her.

I pondered the question. Then I said: "I've been to see a guy." "Who?"

"Someone you should be glad you don't have to meet."

"Is it still that same case?"

"That case? No. That's been shelved. There won't be anything more done about that, unless something turns up."

I could see she was dying to ask about Inger.

"This is something else," I said.

I finished the food and lit up a cigarette. She still hadn't eaten anything.

"Have you started smoking inside?" she asked.

I didn't bother to respond. The nicotine felt good, the smoke rose in front of my eyes, like a cloud to hide behind.

"It makes me nauseous," she said. "You know I can't stand it."

I took a couple of deep drags before stubbing it out on the plate. It looked revolting, the ash and the half-cigarette with clumps of mash around it.

"What has he done?"

"Who?"

"The guy, the nasty one."

"Pretty much everything."

"Like what?"

It surprised me, the interest she was showing, if it wasn't just an excuse to steer the conversation towards the Maria Case again. Or was she asking because she suspected me of lying, of having made up that stuff about another case as a cover? But she suddenly let go of the fork she'd been sitting making patterns in the mashed potato with, letting it sink down into the mash, then she pushed the plate from her with a look of disgust, brought her hands to her forehead and began massaging it with her fingertips.

"What is it?" I asked.

She didn't answer. The rubbing became more feverish.

"I need to go away again," I said, afraid she'd get up at any moment and leave.

She didn't look up, just continued rubbing and pinching her

temples, gritting her teeth, producing a whistling sound as she breathed in and out through them.

"I'll be away for a few days, a week at the most, hard to say.

"Belgrade," I added, since she didn't ask, her current paroxysm made it easy for me, I could say what I wanted, make up any story at all.

"Is it painful?"

Her forehead still bore lines when she took her hand away. She sat there with eyes closed, as though the pain would vanish if she could only manage to remain completely still without moving a muscle.

"I'm leaving tonight," I said. "I'll call you when I know how long I'll be away."

But she didn't seem to be aware of anything around her anymore. The migraines had won out once again, she was listening to them, not me, giving them her full attention, in the hope that if she concentrated long enough she'd discover how to rid herself of them, the pains themselves would whisper confidences in her ear and tell her how to cope, initiate her in their weak points, so that she would be able to put paid to them.

I neglected to tell Inger I could stay over, that the night could last as long as we wanted. I didn't want to think about the time, I just wanted to be there as long as possible, as long as she wanted me to. She took me by the hand as she closed the door behind us, causing a tremble to travel throughout my body. We walked hand in hand along the hall, through the living room and into the kitchen. She asked if I'd like anything. I stroked her hair, she closed her eyes and a sob escaped her. I put my face to hers, breathed in her smell, the salty scent as she opened her mouth and pressed my lips against hers.

We stood like that for a long time.

We went into the bedroom. She undressed and stood in the dim light waiting for me to do the same, which I did, not without a certain clumsiness, but that was of no consequence whatsoever, it didn't matter how it happened as long as it happened. I walked over and kissed her. It was chilly in the room, goose bumps rose up on her skin, which was pale as marzipan and extremely soft, like a silky layer of invisible down. She pushed me over to the bed and lay down on her back with her palms downward. We looked at one another. I bent over her. She began to cry, a pained expression came across her face and tears ran down it. Then she smiled, placed a hand on my shoulder and drew me closer, parting her legs to allow me space. We lay like that for a while, as her face underwent all its changes, she closed her eyes quickly, squeezed them shut tightly, as though in pain, then stared at me terror-stricken, before suddenly beginning to smile, only to cry again. Our genitals were touching, the head of my penis resting against her orifice, as though engaged in a bashful kiss. She ran her hands over my back a few times, then placed one hand on each of my buttocks and pressed gently, until I eased inside. It felt like I grew larger the further in I came. I let out a loud whimper. She gasped. Then the tears started again. We lay like that for a time, without moving, until she lifted her legs, placing one hand behind each knee to spread them wide. She said my name. Insane with desire, I began thrusting as hard as I could.

Afterwards I lay with my head on one of her breasts. I heard the rain through the open window. I didn't know if I was awake or asleep. And while we lay like that, it was as though we started to sink, as if the bed were being pulled down with us in it. The distance between us and the ceiling grew and grew. I tried to raise my arm, but couldn't free it from under a sleeping Inger. And still we sank, the bed continuing its descent, and I thought that all I could do is succumb, let it happen, allow myself to be drawn downward, let it all happen, all come to pass, don't impede it, don't hold on to anything, surrender to the deep, to the swirl and the current, to the rain and the storm, to dreams, to Inger, be there with her, love her and be loved in return. The ceiling continued to float off into the distance. How wonderful: to never get up again, never stress and strain, never work purposefully, never achieve anything, never attempt to make conditions favorable in any particular way.

We were awoken by the intercom buzzer, it was the first time I'd heard it from inside the apartment, a shrill sound like an alarm that had never sounded before. Inger sat up with a start. She sat there looking around confusedly, the duvet clutched to her chest, as if someone had entered the room. She seemed agitated, like an animal that senses danger. It rang again, the button held down longer this time. Inger picked up my shirt, pulled it over her head and jumped out of bed.

"You don't have to answer it," I said.

"Yes I do," she said, still groggy.

She tugged at the bottom of the shirt to make it longer, then tiptoed out of the room. I lay there listening, heard the door on the street being opened, then voices, hers and one more, a man's voice, but it was impossible to make a word out. After a while I heard the click of the latch on the apartment door. Then it went quiet, then voices again. I sat up in bed. The voices grew even clearer, was it because they were raised or because they were drawing closer? The man sounded worked up, I thought I overheard an expletive, and now Inger's voice wasn't to be heard, only his.

I gathered up my clothes, pulled on my trousers and grabbed Inger's sweater from the bedpost on the way out.

Inger was standing in the doorway blocking Halvard, who wanted to enter the living room. On seeing me, she let go of the doorframe and turned her back on him. He stared at me, then Inger, then back at me.

"Can you please leave?" Inger said to him, but he wasn't listening.

"What the fuck is this?" he said, looking at me. "What the fuck's going on?"

He turned to her.

"What the fuck is this?"

"It's none of your business," Inger said, trying to push him back into the hallway.

He brushed her aside and came in my direction, for a moment I was sure he was going to go for me.

"Is that the reason you began snooping around all this again, because you wanted to get into her pants?"

I had no idea what to say.

"Fuck me!" he shouted, and looked at her, then at me, then her, as if he couldn't decide whom he despised more.

"Fuck me!"

"Can you please leave?" Inger repeated.

I figured if I said something, anything at all, it would give him the excuse he needed to punch me.

"Halvard, can you go now?"

He shook his head.

"You heard her," I said.

He stared at me with a crazed grin.

"What's going on?" he asked. "Have you moved in? Do you live here? Is this where you're running your investigation from?"

"Just leave," Inger said, taking hold of his sleeve, her courage regained. "You've no business being here."

He didn't make to move but continued looking at me. I held his stare, ready to intervene if it proved necessary. Then his anger subsided, his body seemed to relax.

"Go," Inger said, her tone milder, recognizing that the danger had passed.

He waited as long as possible before looking away, then he left, Inger followed him out. I heard them speak in low voices in the hallway, then the sound of the door being opened and closed.

Some time passed before she returned. She looked despondent, her face was gray, like it had been the first day I'd been to see her. I approached her and put my arms around her, but she didn't take any notice, just stood there stock-still.

"What did he want?" I asked.

She didn't reply.

I took her hand but she twisted it loose. Her arms hung lifelessly by her sides.

"This is wrong," she said. "We need to stop. It's not right of us."

"Shh," I said, took her by the arm and led her back into the bedroom, the soft, diffuse light in there seeming like it would never fade.

"What is it we're doing?" she asked.

"Come and lie down," I said.

I took off the sweater, got her to sit on the edge of the bed, helped her out of the shirt, her breasts bobbing slightly as they came free, I sat down beside her, kissed her on the shoulder, felt my desire for her growing again, placed a hand on one breast and warmed it.

"What is it we're doing?"

I tried to kiss her but she turned away.

I thought about how it would have been if Halvard hadn't turned up.

Then she snapped out of it. She turned and looked me in the eye.

"What's the point, Kristian? Where can this lead? There can't be anything more than this anyway. It can't be any different than this. The two of us in this room. It can never be anything more than that."

"It doesn't matter," I said. "That's enough for me."

She was about to say something else.

"Please, Inger," I said. "Lie down with me again. Don't think about it anymore. Just lie back down."

She passively allowed me to lay her down flat on the bed. I undressed, my dick unfolding and becoming instantly erect, I tried to avoid it coming into contact with her as I moved her further up the mattress, didn't want her to notice how aroused

I was, and when I lay down beside her I was careful not to let it brush her thigh.

I thought she'd fallen asleep when suddenly she said: "Don't you have to get home?"

I lifted my head and looked at her, she lay staring at the ceiling, as she probably had the entire time.

"No, not yet."

I lay my head back down on her shoulder.

"Do you want me to go?"

It took a while before she answered.

"No. Stay. It's nice lying here like this."

I felt a sudden surge of warmth pass through me when she said that.

"Inger," I said. "I love you."

She didn't reply to that, and after a little while I could tell by her breathing that she'd fallen asleep.

I extricated myself cautiously from her embrace, freed my shirt from the bars in the headboard, and crept out to the living room, where a strange golden-yellow light made it look as if everything in there were under water. It was dark outside, all you could see were some blurry lights far off. There were bottles, glasses, and a few plates stacked on top of one another on the table. One of the bottles had a little left in it. I brought it to my mouth. The wine coursed through me and assuaged a gnawing feeling, making a lump in my throat disappear.

I went over to the writing desk. She had so many framed photographs on display that none were more than partially visible. The frames were in all shapes and sizes, the pictures within both black-and-white and color. Most of them were of Maria, at different ages, some of her as a newborn. There was one of Maria and Inger, taken in a photographer's studio. At the back, completely hidden by the others, in an oval frame, I found a small black-and-white portrait of Inger. The photo had a timeless quality about it, it could have been contemporary or from the late nineteenth century. I tilted it from side to side. Every time the eyes fell upon me I felt a lovely prickling sensation pass through me. Hold this gaze and your journey will never again be in vain.

The telephone rang. Its awful sound slicing through the yellow light and breaking a spell of sorts, I pulled the cord from the wall before it could ring again. I lifted it up. It said *Halvard* on the display. Then the name was replaced by a symbol with an x over it.

I went to the sofa and sat down. A cigarette, which Inger had only taken a few drags of, was sticking out from between two plates. It could still be smoked, what was left of it. The booklet from a CD she'd wanted me to listen to lay on the sofa, the music was Brazilian, a female vocalist. Something black was wedged between the seat cushion and the armrest. I pulled it out. It was Inger's panties. I squeezed them tightly. It was as though they still retained some of her warmth. I raised them to my nose and inhaled. For a moment it was like she was there. I remained sitting with them against my mouth. Then I laid them on the table, and smoothed out the creases, feeling the dampness of the material that had absorbed the moisture from my breath.

I prized a crust loose from the top plate and put it in my mouth. Then I noticed a little drop of wine in one of the other bottles and—feeling like a kid—tried to shake out the very last dregs.

"What are you doing?"

I gave a start. Inger was standing in the doorway, one hand on her shoulder, her hair tousled. Her skin was glowing. The shadow in her crotch resembled an arrow.

I thought about what it was that had brought me here, to her. I considered what it was that had led us to each other. What course had I followed that ended here? There was no course. There was no cause. There was only this, arisen from nothing. A girl who had disappeared, some crumpled-up newspaper slipped inside a pair of wet shoes. There was no direction. I hadn't been on my way anywhere when I met her. Nothing guided me or pulled me along. I'd been drifting. No matter how far back I tried to remember I couldn't recall anything other than this, just my drifting. There'd never been anything that I absolutely had to do. Never anybody I couldn't have done without. Never anyone I feared or had any reason to fear. I'd never been afraid. Not until now, when I saw Inger standing in the doorway and thought that it may not be possible to hold on to her.

"Are you coming?" she asked.

I wanted to say something to her. I wanted to say something that would make it impossible for her to leave me, that would ensure that the connection between us couldn't be broken. My body ached. The few meters between us were enough for me to miss her. I got to my feet. She turned and retreated into the darkness. I followed after her. Life had been in danger of passing me by, but now it had returned, and could finally be mine, unless I let it slip away again.

I didn't know what time of day it was, the room was just as dim, but my heart was pounding, I'd been awoken by something that had scared me, but I couldn't remember what it was, a loud noise, or someone shouting. Inger was still asleep. I leaned over, found my trousers on the floor, took out my mobile and switched it on. It rang almost immediately, even before I'd managed to check the time. I answered it quickly.

It was Risberg.

"Where the fuck are you? What the fuck are you up to? And how the fuck do you expect people to get in touch with you?"

He was hoarse, as though he'd already been shouting for a while.

"What is it?" I asked. My voice was croaky. He could think what he wanted.

It went quiet on the other end of the line. I thought for a moment he wasn't going to say any more, not tell me why he called, that he was going to hold back out of pure resentment. Or was it just that he needed time to compose himself before continuing?

"Maria Danielsen," he said eventually. "We've found her."

Inger was awake, she sat up, rubbed the back of her head with both hands, before brushing her hair back from her face and squinting at me.

I thought about what I could say which wouldn't reveal what we were talking about.

"Where?" I asked.

"Where are you?" he parried.

I gave him the name of a park nearby.

"We'll pick you up in ten minutes," he said and hung up.

I sat there with the mobile in my hand. If I didn't say something, didn't tell her in a normal tone of voice, straight away, that I had to go and take care of something, if I waited just a few seconds more, before saying anything, then she'd understand.

"Kristian," she said. "What is it?"

It was too late. In the space of a few moments it had all returned. Terror gleamed in her eyes. She covered her mouth with her hand.

"They've found a girl," I said.

"No!"

The sound from behind her hand was like that of an animal. I reached for her. She pulled away.

"They don't know if it's Maria," I said.

"No!"

"I'm going to join them out there now."

She opened her mouth and began biting her hand.

"And I'll call you as soon as I know anything."

She tore her hand away, as though she hadn't been the one biting down on it.

"I'm coming with you," she said.

"No, that's not possible."

"I'm coming along," she said.

"You know why you can't."

"I'm coming."

"Inger!"

"I'm coming."

Nobody said anything on the drive out. Risberg and Bernhard had looked at each other as I opened the door; there was also a constable in the car whose name I didn't know. Bernhard had to move over to make room for both of us. They'd probably recognized her the moment they saw her. Possibly managed to make some comments in the short time it took for us to walk over to where the car was waiting. One of them maybe asking, Am I seeing things, or is that the mother? Or, He's not fucking thinking of taking her along, is he? Before the other added, right before I opened the door, Seriously, is he banging her? The rhythm of the wiper on the rear window was irregular, stopping completely at times, before the rubber came loose from the glass and continued on. I wasn't sure how to interpret the fact that nobody had tried to prevent her from coming along. They didn't dare, simple as that. Out of deference for the grief-stricken individual. Besides, it was me they blamed, not her.

I looked at her, without turning my head. It was as if nothing had happened, as though we'd never seen each other naked, nor ever would. It was like we didn't know each other. Like we had never met. Like we saw each other for the first time just a few minutes ago and now, for varying reasons, we were both on our way to the terrible scene that awaited us. As though all contact between us had ceased. If I put my arm around her or touched her, she'd scream and shove me away, or strike me.

The reason being that Maria had returned. Maria had come back and taken her place between us. What had been had existed only in the void Maria had left behind. Now that she was back, now that she was found, there was no longer a place for me, no longer any space where Inger and I could exist.

A patrol car was parked in the cul-de-sac at the end of a winding
forest road. A constable in a black raincoat stood among the trees
a little distance off, further down an incline, and appeared to be
swaying from side to side, as though he had difficulty staying on
his feet. Red-and-white tape was being stretched from the trunk
of one birch tree to the next, looking as though it was being
spun from the black figure. Rain hammered on the roof of the
car. We all remained sitting there for a while, shrinking from
getting out, whether it was the rain or what awaited us that held
us back. Only when the constable had finished fencing off the
area did Risberg turn up his collar and open the door.

The ground was muddy, when you placed your full weight
down your foot slid a little. Somebody holding an umbrella
came running over to us but stood a little way off, uncertain
of whom to offer it to. I placed my hands on Inger's shoulders,
holding tightly for fear of her pushing me away, and signaled
for him to come over to her. I was conscious of Risberg's eyes
on me. He was ready to intervene, ruthlessly and at a moment's
notice, if I didn't do everything by the book from now on. The
sound of rain on the umbrella was like the sound in the car a
few moments ago.

"Wait here!" I called out.

Inger stood with her arms folded, made no move to protest,
merely stared in the direction of the glossy police tape.

"Stay here with her!" I called to the constable, who edged
closer and held the umbrella so as to shelter them both.

We made our way down the hill, the terrain was tricky, like a
large patch of it could come loose at any second and send you
flying into the sludge. The constable in the raincoat raised the
tape so we didn't need to stoop. The incline grew even steeper.
At the bottom, a few meters from the bank of the small lake,
another constable, also wearing a raincoat, was on his knees.

We half-stepped, half-slipped down the last part, Bernhard lost his footing and almost tumbled into the constable. Among the rotten leaves, almost indistinguishable from them, lay a body. It was a girl, her age impossible to estimate, lying exposed with her face down. Everything was the same color as the leaves: her hair, her jacket, if it wasn't a sweater, her buttocks and her legs, which were bare. Another few months and she'd be indistinguishable from the mold and dead leaves. The constable got to his feet and apprised Risberg of the situation, I wasn't really listening; something about who'd reported it and that nothing had been touched since they got here.

There was a scream. One of the other constables had fallen and was sliding downhill on his back, holding a black case up to keep it from landing in the mud. To my horror I saw he was headed for the girl. Before any of us had a chance to react, he flew into her and ended up with his legs splayed over her head and back. His colleague helped him up. He whimpered like a child. Risberg gave him a halfhearted dressing down. High up, at the top of the slope, I could discern the canopy of the umbrella Inger was standing beneath.

The constables opened up the case, assembled the camera equipment, and began taking pictures. They each circled twice, bumping into each other on the steeper terrain, until Risberg gave the word that it was enough. There was a long clap of thunder in the distance, as though somehow provoked by the camera flashes. I tried to light a cigarette, but it disintegrated between my fingers before I managed to spark a flame on the lighter. Risberg, Bernhard, and I looked at one another. Bernhard took a bunch of latex gloves from his pocket and handed us each a pair. Then he hunkered down, bent his torso in an odd fashion, while he placed his fingers on the girl's shoulders and began turning her over, slowly and carefully for fear of the flesh coming away from the bones.

The jacket—it was a jacket—had retained its original color

on the front, green and blue in a sort of checkered pattern, and the zipper on it looked shiny and new. Bernhard looked clearly relieved when he had brought her safely onto her back. He let go of her and took a step back. The skin in her genital area looked unblemished, apart from a few dark patches, her feet, on the other hand, were almost black. Her hair was across her face, covering it completely. Risberg didn't look as if he was planning to assist in any way. I went over to the spot Bernhard had been standing, crouched down, and began taking the hair away from her face.

I don't know if I had a clear image of what Maria looked like before I did it, but I could see right away, even before the face was uncovered, that it wasn't her. I stepped back, stumbled slightly, and had to put my hand in the mud to avoid losing my balance completely.

"Is it her?" I heard Risberg ask.

I straightened up, tore off the soiled latex gloves.

"No," I said. "It's not her."

"Jesus Christ," he groaned.

"Are you sure?" he added, his voice meek.

"Quite sure," I said.

I craned my neck to try and spot the umbrella.

"Quite sure."

"Fuck," Risberg said, then turned to Bernhard. "So who the hell is it?"

I began making my way up the incline. I couldn't see the umbrella anywhere.

Then I caught sight of the constable who'd stayed up there to look after her, coming at full pelt through the trees a little way off. Further down, almost by the water, but closer to us, Inger was running in our direction. I began running towards her, managing to get a hold of her before she made it to the body. She tried to free herself but I used my body weight and we tumbled over and rolled around in the mud.

"It's not her!" I shouted. "Inger! It's not her! It's not her!"

She screamed, thrashing wildly as soon as she got an arm free.

I put my weight on her, pressed her down and held her still. Her body shook. I buried my face in her hair, inhaled through my nose, tried to find her, find my way back to her, hold onto her, the smell of fermented leaves stifling her scent.

"It's not her," I whispered. "You hear me? It's not her."

I don't know how long we lay like that. We were so wet it felt like we had nothing between us, that we lay there naked, stuck to one another, beneath the same jacket, or a tarp. I looked up after a little while. The others were standing looking at us. I got up and tried to pull Inger to her feet, but she made herself as heavy as she could, wouldn't be helped and just remained sitting. I bent down, took her chin in my hand. Black streaks ran down her face. She blinked and blinked.

As I let go, her head sank forward and her hair fell in hanks in front of her face.

I made my way over to the others. The constables had begun taking pictures again, making the corpse's face flash blue, like in a disco.

"What now, Wold?" Risberg said.

He didn't look at me when he spoke but at Inger.

"Where do we go from here?"

Inger was sitting in the same position, her head bowed, almost obscured by the rain, as though she wanted to be consumed by it, by the rain, the mud, all the dead leaves and all the water. Lowered beneath the earth, I thought. But that was the daughter. The mother was still here. She was still alive. Still among us. She was . . . But I didn't allow myself to complete the thought, which would have included the word *mine*.

I didn't feel I had any other choice than to return to the station with Risberg and Bernhard. Inger had gotten a ride with some others. I couldn't be sure, but it was almost like Bernhard derived some kind of pleasure in letting me know he'd found someone to look after her and accompany her home. Even after finishing several hours of work, Bernhard wanted to get started on the missing-person lists as soon as possible, and in a voice that emanated from somewhere other than the sodden body I inhabited, I heard myself offering to help him. What else was I going to do? Where else was I going to go? After all, I was in Belgrade.

Fortunately I had a shirt and a pair of pants in the changing room at work. I peeled off my wet clothes, washed my face and hands, and dried off my entire body as well as I could with paper hand towels. The pile of moist, crumpled-up paper balls in the trash can grew in size. Outside, there was thunder.

Risberg entered while I was dressing. He seemed unsure of himself for once. Like a father, I thought, who doesn't know whether his boy needs a telling-off or moral support.

When he finally opened his mouth, he said: "You realize this cannot continue."

The buttons on my shirt saved me from being at a loss for words. I prepared myself for what was coming.

"After all, you . . . ," he began, but then after stopping to think, said: "We'll deal with it tomorrow.

"When we're better able to," he then added, as though what he had begun had overwhelmed him as he realized the extent of it.

"Okay," I said.

"Right," he said, turned, and left. I glanced in the mirror but couldn't manage to associate anything with the face I saw. The dry clothes felt unfamiliar. Socks were the only thing I hadn't found, and I had an odd sensation as I walked barefoot down the corridor, the linoleum sticking to the soles of my feet in short flaps of cold, of feeling like a guest, in borrowed clothes, who had just awoken from their first night under the roof of a host.

I stopped by my own office on my way to Bernhard's. My chair felt strange, adjusted for someone else to sit in. I gave a start when I went to swing my feet back and they came into contact with the cold steel base. I found a stray cigarette in one of the drawers. I could hardly wait to get it lit.

I wondered who it was that had driven Inger home. I mulled over what he'd been ordered to do. To set her off just outside number 18? Or to accompany her to the door? Or follow her all the way up? Or go inside and wait a while. Stay overnight, perhaps, if she so wished?

Some newspaper clippings were pinned to the corkboard above the desk, one from a tabloid with a photo of me and Bernhard standing shoulder to shoulder, our arms folded, looking like we thought we were hard as nails, whereas it was the photographer who'd instructed us on how to pose, while we, pleased with the attention, had willingly cooperated. The headline read: NORWEGIAN POLICE ASSIST INTERPOL. Beneath the picture, it said: *Norwegian police investigators Kristian Wold (41) and Bernhard Meyer (42) have both played a central part in the exposure of an international human-trafficking ring.*

Kristian Wold (41). There it was again. The parentheses. The hedge clippers. I too will die, I thought. I too will disappear. In a sense I too am already gone, already dead.

3

Siting back behind the wheel didn't fill me with the feeling I'd been looking forward to, even though everything was in perfect order, the car washed outside and vacuumed inside, everything that had been lying around gathered up and neatly placed in the pockets of the doors, instead it gave me the feeling of it having been stolen, of someone having fiddled around with it, of having no way of knowing what the people who had taken possession of it had been up to. The engine sounded different too, but that was probably only because it had been overhauled.

I drove the car from the garage up to the parking lot of a newly refurbished restaurant farther up the hill, which, on a clear day, offered a vista over the entire city and port area, although the view which was afforded to me now resembled more a sort of panoramic porridge. I sat in the car and smoked two cigarettes. The windshield misted up. I called Inger but got no answer. So I wrote her a text and sent it: *Are you there? Could you answer the phone? I need to talk to you. K.* While I was waiting I opened my inbox. The last message I'd received from her was over a week old. I brought it up on the screen, even though I knew it only contained a solitary smiley, a yellow face in the center of a tiny sunflower.

I waited a quarter of an hour, then started the engine and pulled out. My mobile beeped while I was driving through some traffic lights, I fumbled in my pocket but it had snagged in the lining and I couldn't get hold of it. A horn blared. I looked up. A car was coming right at me. I swerved, the right front wheel hit the curb, the car lurched onto the sidewalk with a jump and then stopped. The driver behind me honked his horn as well and then pulled out and drove past. I tore the phone loose from my pocket and unlocked it. The text was from Anne-Sofie. I couldn't face opening it and reversed off the sidewalk, where two old men stood shaking their fists, and drove on.

I parked in front of the newsstand on the far side of the road. There was a light on in the kitchen but not the living room. I called her number, thought I saw someone move up there but wasn't certain. I let it ring out before I hung up.

There was an ambulance in front of the entrance. A small group of people had formed. After a while, two men in yellow raincoats came up the basement steps carrying a stretcher. The one in front tried unsuccessfully to hook the ambulance door open with his foot. One of the onlookers came to his aid and held the door while the man with the hearing aid, it must have been him, was slid in on the stretcher. Another man in yellow emerged from the basement steps carrying a white case in his hand.

The onlookers lingered for a while after the ambulance departed. It looked like they were listening to something the man who had held the door was saying, the assistance he'd offered having no doubt conferred him some standing in their eyes, making what he had to tell them of interest.

I tried ringing once more.

I pictured Inger sitting in a chair with the telephone in front of her, waiting for it to stop ringing. What did she think when she thought of me? Or was I already absent from her thoughts? Everything, all we had, erased in favor of Maria, that one emotion that stifled all others, making it impossible to long for anything else. I peered up at the row of windows. Where was she? Going from room to room, walking round in circles, or sitting still—inactive, paralyzed again? The fact that it hadn't been her we found that day after all, had that been like losing her all over again? Was she back where she had been? Facing a terror that didn't allow her to think of anything else? A terror from which only Maria, alive or dead, could release her?

I gave the cigarette pack on the dash another shake. Then I ran my hand under the seat and groped around, but if there had been any left in the pack I found lying there it was safe to assume someone at the garage had helped themselves to them.

The thrumming on the roof became more of a rumble when I opened the car door. Fortunately the newsstand wasn't too far to walk and the downpour had yet to penetrate its rotten awning. The man behind the counter, who may actually not have been the owner, as I'd previously thought, seemed surprised when I told him what brand I wanted. Somebody bumped into me, causing me to drop the change he handed me, then swore and was gone before I managed to turn around. The pavement was covered with flattened splodges of chewing gum, putting me in mind of the pattern of Anne-Sofie's summer dress. It was raining so heavily I had difficulty recognizing my own car, and it was impossible to see if it was empty or if someone was still sitting inside.

The inside of the car smelled like another man, unfamiliar sweat mingled with pungent tobacco, like someone had been living in it for weeks. I held my breath as I got in, then rolled down the window and lit up a cigarette. The smell wafted over my face. Everything, even the seat I was sitting in, felt moist.

I rolled up the window, turned the ignition, and switched on the fan. The warm blast smelled of burned plastic. I put on the windshield wipers and watched the people emerging from the subway station in a mixture of blurry and distinct shapes. Nearly all of them began to run as soon as they were out, as though fleeing from something underground. It was impossible to imagine any of them consumed by passion.

Anne-Sofie was pacing back and forth in the living room when I came home. She didn't answer me when I spoke to her, didn't look in my direction, just tramped round and round, driven by a tremendous surplus of energy, a surplus without any outlet, which couldn't be put to any use and therefore ended up in this unpleasant, prolonged waltz.

"Do you think I'm stupid?" she suddenly shouted. "Or is it just because you don't give a shit whether I find out or not? Do you think I don't know what's going on? Do you think I'm oblivious to everything? Do you actually believe that I'm so thick I don't get it?"

"What?" I asked.

She paused for a moment, stared around the room wildly, then continued stamping around.

"Can't you hear what I'm saying? Can't you hear what I'm saying?"

Then she screamed: "Can't you hear what I'm saying?!"

"I hear what you're saying," I said. "But I don't know what you mean."

"Oh yes you do. You know very well what I mean. But you won't answer. You won't answer because you know exactly what it's about."

"What's it about?" I replied, feeling gratification at dragging it out, resisting all her efforts and making it impossible for her to get anywhere.

She continued pacing around the room.

"Can you give me a proper answer?" she yelled. "Can you give me a proper answer?"

"If you know about something," I said, "and I don't

understand what it is, then you have to be the one who explains it to me."

Finally she halted.

"I've read your text messages," she said. "I've read what she writes to you."

I wanted to say something, but the anger that flared up turned immediately to fatigue, the rage extinguished before it had time to catch flame.

I waited for a moment, then I said: "In that case there's nothing else you need to know, is there?"

"So you admit it?"

"What?"

"That you're having an affair with her," she said, her tone abruptly mild.

"Who?"

Her irritation was no match for my patience, I knew that: it felt like we could keep going on like this for an eternity, back and forth over the same thing.

"Where do you meet?" she asked.

I turned to leave but she grabbed hold of me. "What do you do when you're together? What do you talk about?"

I stood motionless. She was incandescent.

"What do you talk about?" she screamed.

Then in a lower voice: "What do you say to her? What do you say when you meet her? What's the first thing you say when the two of you meet?"

Her thoughts were all over the place, that was obvious, being pulled here, then there, and not finding anywhere to rest.

"What about her daughter? Have you stopped looking for her?"

I made to leave but she held me tightly.

"You're probably not that interested in finding her anymore, now that you have her?"

"Anne," I said.

All her features were in constant motion.

"So while the pair of you fuck each other she's left to fend for herself? Is that how it is?"

I twisted free with a jerk. She swayed on her feet.

"While you and the mother fuck each other," she said, "is there someone else fucking her?"

Her mouth opened and closed like a little animal in the middle of her white, blurry face.

"And neither of you give a shit about that, as long as you can fuck each other?"

Before I knew what I was doing she was on the floor floundering. She got up and launched herself at me. I hit her again, this time she stumbled backwards but managed to stay on her feet. A purple patch had appeared on one cheek, right under her eye. The sight of it made me feel good: finally, at least one thing that had got through to her. She brought her hand to her cheek. I took a step towards her but she recoiled. Her eyes were wide. One of her socks had fallen off and her cardigan was in disorder, one shoulder bare and a breast showing. She looked like the hooker from the hotel.

"I'll do it again," I said.

My fingers ached as I unclenched my fist.

"I swear, I'll do it again, if I have to."

Torches had been placed in the gravel along the length of the driveway, ready to be lit when darkness fell, and large pots with fresh flowers stood on either end of the steps up to the front door. A young man in a footman's uniform opened before I had a chance to ring.

"Are you here to deliver the wine?" he asked.

I showed him my badge.

"I have an appointment with Gunerius," I said, lying.

He let me in.

"Just a moment."

His clothes made him look like a servant from the turn of the twentieth century, his gait like a lout from this one. It took a while for him to return, when he finally did he told me it would be some time before Gunerius was available, and if I liked I could betake myself to the reception room where I could also have something to drink. I declined both offers and ruminated on the phrase, *betake myself to the reception room*. But perhaps part of his contract stipulated he had to use archaic words and expressions when addressing the hosts or their guests? Then it struck me that he probably wasn't part of the household, that he'd been rented for the occasion, that it might well have been the first time he wore a servant's uniform, and that perhaps he was the son of an acquaintance of theirs, hired to play the role of a lackey and yet to learn his lines properly.

I began to regret not allowing him to show me into the reception room: the door was open and I could hear sounds from within that piqued my curiosity, a clinking, followed by a squeaking sound, then silence, until the clinking returned and the squeaking a moment later. Eventually I couldn't resist going

over to the doorway and looking inside. It was a large room,
glittering with chandeliers and crystal. There was a long table
in the middle of the room, covered in a white tablecloth, with
place settings for twenty or thirty people. Mrs. Gunerius was
dressed up and seated in a wheelchair at the far end. She was
arranging knives, forks, and spoons with very slow, deliberate
movements. When she'd laid down one set, she took hold of the
wheels, trundled around the corner to the next place setting,
and in the same methodical fashion began taking cutlery from
a large case placed across the arms of the wheelchair.

I withdrew before she had a chance to notice me. Gunerius
appeared through a door at the far end of the hall. The shirt he
was wearing was so brilliantly white that it gave his complexion
an almost mauve tinge. He muttered aloud as he approached,
fiddling with the end of one shirtsleeve.

He walked right over to me before looking up. To my surprise, he smiled, though the sarcasm in his voice was obvious.

"Ah!" he groaned. "Would you mind?"

He held up the shirtsleeve in front of me and passed me a
silver cufflink with his other hand. I felt oddly subservient while
I fastened it for him, then annoyed at myself for having just gone
along with it.

"Thank you," he said, studying the result, plainly satisfied.
He looked at me with surprise.

"Weren't you offered a drink?"

"I was, thank you," I said.

His burly build was overwhelming at close quarters. It was
impossible to imagine a conversation where he wasn't the dom-
inant party.

"Well?" he said cheerfully. "How can I help you?"

He put an emphasis on *I* and *you*, as though he considered
himself obliged to return the favor.

"I've been to see Maltek," I said.

"Maltek?" he replied, without evincing any reaction
whatsoever.

"Your friend."

"My friend?"

"What term would you use yourself?"

He repeated the name a few times, as if hoping the taste of it in his mouth would provide the answer as to what or who he was.

I became aware of the squeaking sound again, now coming from behind me. I turned. Mrs. Gunerius came wheeling towards us with her legs raised in front like a battering ram.

"Table set?" Gunerius asked.

She passed me, performing an elegant arc that brought her to a stop by her husband's side: she had complete control of her vehicle.

"It's our annual dinner," Gunerius said. "The mayor is coming. The police commissioner as well."

The pride he took in telling me this was as apparent as his pleasure.

"The cover charge is 20,000."

He smiled. Both of them looked like they were posing for a photograph.

"Money which goes directly to the Salvation Army," Mrs. Gunerius said.

Once again, the somber, sonorous voice bursting from the frail frame caught me off guard.

He placed his hand on her shoulder.

"It was Tove's idea," he said. "No one believed it could be done, myself included. Now we're into our fifth year."

"Sixth," she corrected.

"Now people fight for the privilege. We've had to put a cap on the number of guests. There's only so much space after all, even in a house like this!"

Music began to play above us, which I recognized after a moment as the same aria I had heard the first time I'd been there. I glanced at Gunerius but his face gave nothing away. For a moment I was in doubt as to whether I'd actually been there before, and whether he was the same man who had stood in front of me in a robe with his dick dangling exposed.

"Perhaps the Inspector . . . ," he began, switching between looking at me and at his wife.

Mrs. Gunerius knitted her brows.

"We could always manage to make room for one more," he said. "If you would care to join us?"

"I don't think so," I said. "But thank you."

"Free of charge obviously!" he laughed. "On the house, so to speak."

Even though I knew Mrs. Gunerius would remain in our company until I left, I still couldn't bring myself to continue my questioning of her husband as long as she was.

At the same time I was taken aback by their tone towards each other, so at odds from what I would have imagined beforehand, as though she had authority over him, like a mother with an unruly child. There was something quite contradictory in the impression they gave as a couple, him so imposing and her so fragile. Their strength seemed inversely proportional to their size.

And it struck me that the reason for her staying put was not because she'd obediently taken up her place by his side, but because she wanted to listen to what was being said, to establish how much I'd managed to find out, while at the same time ensure that her husband, the oversized child, didn't disclose anything that might sully their reputation. She was there because she didn't believe he could handle the situation, because she didn't want to risk losing control. She had come over as soon as she heard our voices. She didn't want to miss a word we said. She sat there, ready to intervene if it proved necessary. All set to step in should the situation require it.

And it also occurred to me that this was the reason I'd never get anywhere with either of them. Because she'd already forgiven him, the big child that he was. Because she knew which of them was stronger. Just as she'd forgive him all the future misery he'd cause, all his unfortunate impulses and malicious acts. She sat there, an incorruptible guardian, at the side of the man who had tried to cut her leg off, without expressing anything other than cool contempt for anything or anybody that could pose a conceivable threat to the marital regime which on the face of it he ran, but in reality she oversaw.

The doorbell rang from somewhere in the house. The footman appeared after a few moments, strode to the front door and opened it wide. Two men entered, each carrying a case of wine. The lackey went ahead and showed them the way. Then the doorbell sounded once more. Again he appeared, running this time. He looked over at the hosts and raised his arms in a despairing gesture.

"Hang in there, Magnus!" Gunerius called out.

I realized I wasn't going to get anywhere. Their world was closed to any further intrusion. All of it: the torches along the driveway, the big flowerpots, shirt cuffs, the jewelry, the set table, the deliveries, the bustle around them, all of it like armor between them and me.

A line of men in red-checked pants and white chef's hats went by in the background, all carrying enormous platters covered with tinfoil. It looked like an advertisement. Meanwhile, the Guneriuses were directly in front of me, patiently waiting for me to finish up and leave. They stood there dressed in their finest, holding the line and letting nothing weaken them. They would continue as before, both of them. No one on earth could stop them. Nothing could alter them, the path they were set upon, or the cooperation they were prepared to commit to. It was worth so much, the alliance they formed, that nothing could create discord between them. Everything would run its course. She would maintain the control she had over him until something caused him to explode and he took it out on her again. Then he would beg her forgiveness, which would be forthcoming, and she would again regain her power, until the next time he flew into a rage. The only times she had control over him was when he lost it himself. He was the child, an obedient one at that, and all the deference made him fly off the handle now and then, like an airing of sorts, a necessary cleansing perhaps, a type of purging. Once in a while she feared him, and with good reason: otherwise not at all. Otherwise she had him where she wanted him. And I imagined that it must be a relief for him, with so many people under his thumb, being the only person under hers.

Sitting in the car at my usual spot by the newsstand opposite number 18, I was reminded of the interminable hours that used to crawl along on stakeouts back in my first few years in uniform. And I still hadn't seen any sign of her, not in the windows, nor on her way in or out of the building. It was like she wasn't there any longer, like she too had vanished.

I wondered if that was what had happened in the woods that day: her last hope of finding Maria had been taken from her. And at the same time as she surrendered all hope she also relinquished whatever remained connecting her to the outside world.

I thought about how the reason she didn't answer my calls, the reason she didn't show herself, didn't want anything more to do with me, was because I was part of that world she no longer had cause to have anything to do with.

And I pondered how that was the reason she had wanted to be with me all the same, that in me she had found a link to Maria and to the hope of finding her, and by being close to me had felt closer to Maria, as close as it was possible to get, and that she, although I believed, or chose to believe, that she didn't, had in reality thought about Maria every minute, every second we'd been together.

What if it had been Maria lying there, I thought, beginning to decompose into the ground, what would have happened with us then? Would she have thanked me, and then have been done with me, not so much as offer me a single thought, or dignify me with a word or look from that moment on? Or would our relationship have endured, precisely because I was the one who had led her to her daughter, had guided her out of anxiety and despair to a certainty, which although horrible, was still a release of sorts, which granted her some measure of peace? Would she then, in the fullness of time, have been able to love me?

I had tried ringing her from a pay phone, I had an idea it was me she didn't want to talk to and if the call came from an unknown number she'd take it. And sure enough, after a couple of rings I heard her voice on the other end of the line. But I couldn't bring myself to say anything, dismayed as I was by the confirmation of my suspicions, I just stood there with the receiver in my hand, began to shake and felt her presence fill the whole of the narrow glass box I was in, and she must have realized who it was, because after saying "hello?" twice she hung up.

My mobile rang. It was Anne-Sofie, a milder tone to her voice than usual.

"Are you on your way?" she asked.

"Yes," I said, and felt cold inside, "I won't be long."

"Okay, well get a move on," she said, something that was so unfamiliar and so unnecessary for her to say, that I sat for a while afterwards mulling over what it might conceivably signify.

I started up the engine and looked up one last time at the row of windows. Just then someone came out the front door of the building, a man I quickly recognized: it was Halvard Vendelbo. He opened a green umbrella and set off hurriedly in the direction of the parking lot across the street. I considered running after him and grabbing hold of him before he made it to his car. I waited instead until the blue Fiesta stopped at the exit to the road and flashed its turn signal. I pulled out and followed him, two cars between my own and his. A reflector on the rear window made the car easy to tail. He got on the freeway, heading towards the football stadium at first, but at the roundabout by the hospital he made a left and headed in the direction of the University area. The two cars between us disappeared, the reflective sticker shone bright and wet in the rain, which was cleaved steadily into viscous flashes by my windshield wipers, working away with a plaintive sound.

A short side road off another roundabout led to the first high-rise building on the campus, named, if memory serves, after a famous mathematician. He pulled over and left his lights on. I parked twenty meters behind and turned mine off. Not long after, a woman appeared in a white coat holding the collars up. She jogged the last few meters to Vendelbo's car, the door opened for her before she reached it and she got inside. I pictured the little round stomach beneath the white raincoat that the rain now dripped off before forming a little puddle at her feet. Was she a student or a teacher? She could just as likely be one as the other. But why didn't he pull out? Did she have something to tell him and he wanted to give her his undivided attention? Or were they quarrelling? Was she starting to suspect something, was she grilling him about where he'd been, if he'd been at Inger's again and what exactly he'd been up to there?

I considered going over, getting into the backseat, to their shared astonishment, like a messenger from out of nowhere, and ask him, so she could hear it, exactly what business he had at his ex-wife's place. Or should I wait and do it anonymously, call her and intimate that it might not be a bad idea to ask him what kind of relationship still existed between him and Inger?

How was he able to do it, leave one and go straight to the other?

I took out my mobile and called Inger's number, keeping my eyes fixed on the luminous little patch on the rear window while I listened to the distant tone.

And still the two of them remained sitting in the car, as though there were no end of things to clear up before they could get going.

I didn't dare ring the buzzer and pretended instead to be searching for a name. I let my eyes run down the whole column, her name was the hardest to make out, scrawled in ballpoint on a scrap of paper stuck behind the little dirty plastic window, so unlike the meticulously rendered signage on the post box inside. Moreover, only her name appeared on the doorbell outside, not Maria's. Why? I placed my fingers on the smooth plastic. The doorbell had decoration around it that made it resemble a fountain.

There was a solid clicking sound. I felt the rush of air as the door was opened, a moment later I was inside and making my way up the stairs, so quickly that I doubted the people on their way out had even noticed someone slipping past them.

I was reluctant to ring and knocked instead, telling myself that would make it harder for her not to open.

I rapped on the door several times but no one answered.

And then I felt a tightening and tiredness in my temples that seemed to send a wave of fatigue throughout my entire body. I leaned back against the wall and slid down until I was sitting on the floor, which was ice cold.

I didn't know how long I'd been sitting there when I heard the door downstairs opening, followed by a rattle from the mailboxes, then footsteps on the stairs. I wanted to get to my feet but I didn't have the energy.

As the footsteps grew closer I could tell they weren't hers.

A woman appeared bearing two full-looking shopping bags. She held me in her peripheral vision but tried not to show it.

She'd hardly disappeared up to the next floor when I heard the door below opening again. This time the person ascending the stairs did it more swiftly and it wasn't long before I saw Inger's head between the balusters. I hurried to get to my feet. She saw me but didn't slow her pace, not before halting at the door. She put down a shopping bag.

"Hi," she said, giving away so little one way or the other that the feeling of despair I had in my chest moved up to my throat.

"Hi," I replied.

She took out the key and unlocked the door. When she stepped inside I remained in the hallway. She didn't ask me in, nor did she refuse me entry.

She left the door open. I could hear her taking her coat off. I went inside.

"Can you close the door?" she asked.

Her voice was so bland, it sounded like there wasn't a flicker of life left in her. She picked up the bag and disappeared.

Should I remove my shoes? Should I hang up my jacket? Should I wait until she returned and we'd had a chance to talk about how things should be? Did I have any rights, was I part of her life or was I an outsider again?

I heard her moving around in the kitchen. But when I went in she was just standing there, looking listless and facing the sink. I put my arms around her and buried my head in her hair. She didn't do anything, neither spoke nor responded in any other way. I hugged her tightly but realized no reaction was forthcoming.

I let go of her. She turned around. I wanted her to say something but knew she wasn't about to, not before I opened my mouth.

"What about us?" I said. "What happens to us now?"

I didn't recognize my own voice.

She stroked my cheek.

"I don't know," she said, in a hushed tone. "I don't know."

"I can't . . ." I began, but had no idea what I wanted to say.

She put her arms around me. I met her embrace and clung to

her tightly. Finally I felt her, her body against mine, no longer resistant. I found her face, pressed my lips against hers. I knew I had to have her. Whether she wanted to or not, I had to have her. She opened her mouth, but just a little, not with enough desire and only because I forced her. It was a bite more than a kiss.

Then she tensed up again.

I loosened my hold.

"I don't know, Kristian," she said. "It's so confusing. I can't make sense of things. I don't know what anything is anymore."

"Do you need to know what it is?" I asked.

"You have to give me time. I can't give you any answers right now."

"I can wait," I said. "I'll wait as long as you like."

She smiled. "You're sweet. And kind," she said.

I didn't want to say it but it was already on the way out and impossible to stop. "What about Halvard?"

"What do you mean?"

"What about you and Halvard? Are you as unsure about that?"

"Kristian, what do you mean?"

"Are you uncertain about what that is as well? He was just here, wasn't he?"

The faintest shadow of something crossed her face.

We stood for a while without speaking.

"You should go," she said finally.

It sounded like she was standing far away when she said it.

"You should go. Okay?"

She raised her hand.

"You need to leave. You can't be here. You understand?"

The receptionist gave a start when he caught sight of me. He hastened to stick something beneath the pile of papers in front of him before getting to his feet, after which he was more than obliging.

"The girl in room 214," I said.

"Rita?" he asked.

"Yeah, maybe," I said. "Is she there now?"

"Yes," he said and glanced at his watch. "But there's someone with her."

I took the steps two at a time, heard the receptionist say something but didn't catch what. The door was locked. I jiggled the handle, banged loudly, said it was the police and shouted for it to be opened immediately. The frantic activity within was obvious from the hallway. Then the door opened. Rita was wearing the same robe as last time, her hair was tousled, and it may have been due to the lighting in the hall but she seemed older, her jowls were more prominent and she had dark rings under her eyes.

At first she assumed a defiant expression. I pushed the door open. Over by the bed, a middle-aged man was busy buttoning his shirt, beads of perspiration on his brow, on seeing me he released a gasp.

Rita asked what the fuck I was thinking, bursting in like that. I ignored her, approached her customer and flashed my badge, allowed him to sweat a little first then told him to scoot on home to his wife and kids.

He hurried out, looking like a man who had evaded a death sentence.

Rita swore. I turned to her.

"Who the fuck's going to pay me now?" she asked, miffed. "You?"

On seeming to recognize me she mellowed slightly.

"Rita?" I asked.

"Yeah?"

She regained her composure, closed the door and put her back to it. Her robe was almost the same color as her skin, making her appear naked even in that.

"What do you want?" she asked.

"You usually work from here?"

She thought the question over.

"So what if I do?"

"Who do you work for?"

"Nobody," she said. "Myself," she added.

"And the other girls?"

"Themselves," she said, with a sigh of resignation, as though it were the most idiotic question anyone could ask her.

"And you expect me to believe that?" I said.

I took out my cigarettes and offered her one.

"No thanks."

I could see she wanted one by the way she followed mine with her eyes, watching as I put it between my lips, and I made a conscious effort to take my time as I lit it up, taking the first deep drag with demonstrative pleasure.

"How is he?" she asked.

"Who?"

"Him," she said, taking hold of her wrist.

"He's fine," I said. "He'll be all right."

She looked nervous. No doubt awaiting the bad news she assumed I'd come to convey.

"He won't be bothering you anymore," I said.

"And what about me?"

I waited a little before replying.

"I've buried that," I said. "I can't promise you anything, but it should be okay."

She looked surprised, before her momentary relief gave way to a slight narrowing of her eyes.

"So why are you here?" she asked.

There was a hint of fear in her voice.

I brought my hand to my nose, inhaled the scent of Inger, of her hair, her mouth. Rita's guard was up, I could see it in her eyes, like a soldier standing sentry, prepared for any eventuality.

Then her features relaxed, and she smiled.

"Same as last time?"

I'm not sure how, but as soon as I shut the door behind me I knew the apartment had been cleaned, that the clutter that had accumulated over such a long time had been tidied away, an old order restored. From the kitchen I heard the sloshing of the washing machine. Water in here as well, I thought. Water everywhere. I hung up my jacket and went in the living room. Anne-Sofie's sewing machine was the only thing out, beside which lay a pile of patterns and some folded material. It put me in mind of Halvard Vendelbo's living room. It seemed like she'd even gotten around to the drinks cabinet, the bottles looked like they had been lined up. I poured myself a brandy, knocked it back and poured another. My eyes were drawn to the crack in the wall beneath the picture. It looked like a wound with a border of clotted blood. I touched it with my fingertips and the wallpaper gave a little, as though there were nothing behind.

I walked over to the door of the balcony and pulled the curtain back. A round wooden table with flaps stood outside, covered in mold, one corner of the green outdoor mat it stood upon curled upwards. I turned the key, opened the door slightly and took out my cigarette pack. I thought about how long it had been since I'd been alone in the apartment. Then I tried to imagine Inger here, picture her sitting in one of the chairs, in front of the mirror in the bathroom, or by the worktop in the kitchen, or else that when I turned around in a moment she'd come walking across the living room towards me, but it was like I couldn't hold on to both thoughts, as though one excluded the other: when I thought about the rooms in the apartment she was lost to me, and when I thought about her the rooms disappeared.

I drank from the glass, held the brandy in my mouth for a

long time and listened to the ticking of the cuckoo clock on the wall.

What was going on between Inger and Halvard? He still seemed to exert an influence over her. The way he'd come in to the apartment that day. As though it were still his. How often was he there? What did they do when he was? Why did she let him in and not me? Did they have some prearranged signal? Were they having an affair, unbeknownst to me or to Kristina?

But he had precedence, by virtue of what had been, of what had happened. He could come and go in her life for a while yet. What was it he was after? Why didn't he let go of Inger the same way he'd let go of Maria? Was he finished with his daughter but not with his ex-wife?

The suspicion was suddenly there again, as terrible as it might be: that he had done it, he had abducted Maria and killed her, so that he could be alone with Inger. That it had been his plan, to get rid of what stood between him and Inger, to unite in grief, to resume the relationship they'd had prior to family life ruining it, to find their way back to how things had been before Maria came into the world.

I heard something from out in the hall.

"Kristian?"

I waited to answer until she came into view, appearing in the doorway with a coat on and a basket of clothes under her arm.

"I was down in the laundry room."

"How are things?" I asked, hearing how stupid it sounded but unable to think of anything else.

"I went to see Fretheim today," she said.

"Oh really?"

She put down the basket and came into the living room. The bruising under her eye was covered with make-up but was still visible, like a brown patch on an apple.

"He gave me some new tablets. I took one while I was there. And do you know what?"

She came right over to me.

"I can't feel a thing. All the pains are gone."

"That's great," I said. "Maybe they might work."

I drained my glass, the alcohol felt like it had dislodged part of my brain.

"They're already working," she said. "Maybe they'll go away for good. Imagine if they do, Kristian. Imagine they disappear for good."

She took hold of my arm. I didn't know what to do. I twisted loose, went over to the bar and picked up the bottle.

"What is it?" Anne-Sofie asked.

"What do you mean?"

I poured myself a glass.

"Is something wrong?"

"No."

"You seem strange."

"It's nothing. Just tired."

She seemed unsure of what to say.

"Imagine," she said. "Imagine it goes away. Imagine it works."

"Let's hope so," I said. No matter how I tried, I couldn't lend my voice a lively tone.

"What's with you?" Anne-Sofie asked. "Are you drunk?"

"I have to head out again," I said.

"You can't drive now."

I took out my cigarettes and stood at the balcony door, took pleasure in the smoke, the thrumming of the rain, the water inundating everything, the celestial tank that never ran dry. Inger was out there somewhere. Halvard and Kristina were out there. So was Maria. And Rita.

"I thought we might eat out," I heard from behind me, her voice was feeble, as though she didn't believe there was any chance herself.

"I have to do something first," I said.

"Can't it wait?"

She came over to me, placed her hand on my shoulder, then leaned against my back, slipping her hands under my arms, around my torso and holding me tight.

"Please."

I had to fight an overwhelming urge to tear free, push her away, I felt a rising nausea as she hugged me tighter, didn't know which leg to put my weight on, didn't know what to do with my arms, considered for a moment flinging the brandy glass at the window as hard as I could, longed to hear something smash and see it break into pieces.

She wouldn't let go. I stood motionless and thought about how this was the last time we'd have anything to do with each other. That after she let go of me I knew I'd never let her near me again. There was nothing more I could say, nothing more we could do. I felt sorry for her, but that was all I felt.

How much shit can a man take and still believe he's headed in the right direction? There was nobody manning the reception at the Majestic. A radio was playing. I tapped the brass call bell but it only produced a dull click. I leaned over the counter: a pile of papers, some polystyrene McDonald's boxes, and a porn magazine with a glossy cover. I walked around, squatted down and checked the underside of the desk, where a Smith & Wesson .38 and a baseball bat were held in place by an artful system of bent nails. I stood up again and surveyed the receptionist's clutter. The woman on the cover of the magazine was beaming despite having a dick in every orifice. I slipped it beneath some papers. Who actually gets turned on by grinning women?

At the rear of the reception room a door stood ajar. I pushed it open and entered a narrow hallway. The music grew louder and I realized the radio was somewhere farther back and not in the reception room. At the end of the hallway I heard a trickling sound coming from behind a door on the right, where someone had spray-painted *UP YOURS* followed by a telephone number. The door led to a room that turned out to be bigger than I had expected. Upon entering, the interior almost overwhelmed me, causing me to sway slightly and place my hand on the doorframe for support. Everything inside was green, all the tiles on the floor, the ceiling, and the walls, the rows of sinks in the center, the shower stalls and toilet cubicles, all in the same sickly shade of green, pumping like a heart in the flicker of a faulty fluorescent tube on the ceiling. A long mirror formed a partition between the two rows of sinks, reflecting the green from everything around it. As I drew closer the filth became more apparent, not one clean surface was to be seen and I could observe that in actual fact the green light was reflected on some large discs of filth that appeared to be all over the once shiny surface. The sinks, I now saw, were also completely covered. Even the floor tiles were caked with mottled lumps of dirt or mold.

I looked behind me and saw that the doors and walls were also coated with the substance, patches of which resembled left-over food, and it was only then I noticed the stench in there, as though it had waited for me to come right into the room before revealing itself. I took a deep breath and was about to leave when I heard someone clear their throat. I stood there, registered the clink of a belt buckle and then the flush of a toilet from one of the cubicles.

I breathed through my mouth. The throbbing room made my stomach turn. One of the cubicle doors opened. At first I thought it was the old man from the basement flat in number 18, because he walked with legs wide apart, as though frozen in the position I'd seen him sitting in. But it wasn't him, it was a gangly Vietnamese man, his face and clothes bathed in green, who grimaced upon catching sight of me. He grinned, scratched his crotch with an exaggerated gesture then tottered over to one of the sinks. It looked like some invisible joist was forcing his knees apart. I waited until he disappeared behind the mirror, only free to leave, I told myself, when I couldn't see him anymore, or when he couldn't see me. Still, I felt certain he'd come after me when I turned to go. I tensed and prepared myself to hear a deafening noise from behind, or feel something cold plunge into my back.

I hurried out and went through the door at the end of the hallway, which led to a stairwell. There were voices coming from above. I walked up two flights of steps and realized I was on my way into the rear entrance of the Majestic. The voices grew louder. It was difficult to say whether they testified to pleasure or pain. On the third floor, I found myself in the hallway where Rita's room was. I walked to her door and knocked. No answer.

I knocked again. Still no sound. I tried the door, felt my anger growing as I discovered that it was locked, that it wasn't possible to get in. I called out her name several times. A door opened further down the hall, then another. I didn't bother to turn around. I pounded on the door a few more times, then took a step back, placed my foot against the lock plate and kicked with all my strength.

The entire jamb on the frame came free as the door flew open. The room was empty, left in the mess that probably always prevailed. All the same I took a look around, going as far as getting down on the floor and checking under the bed, just in case she was somewhere in the room, lying or huddled someplace, quiet as a mouse, holding her breath and waiting for me to leave.

I looked over at the oval mirror on the wardrobe. At first the door vibrated but then the image came to rest. I wasn't a pretty sight. My jacket was covered in stains, my hair was sticking up on one side and a slight bulge in the glass made my skin merge where one of my eyes should have been. I walked over to the wardrobe and opened both doors. Coats and dresses hung inside, looking like a line of trees, like a little world all its own. But no Rita. No Rita anywhere.

The cop at the front desk had worked the stint long enough to recognize me, but he hadn't gotten wind of my suspension. He swallowed my story about the keycard without question. I didn't run into any familiar faces en route to Bernhard's office either, and the people I did meet were too busy to notice me. Bernhard, on the other hand, craned his neck to gawp around me when I stuck my head in his door, as though to check if anyone else was behind me, and even after I'd closed the door he went over, opened it a crack, and took an extra look. He was nervous but he did his best to hide it.

"What are you doing here?" he asked.

"I need help," I said.

"What kind of help? If Risberg sees you here . . ."

"Fuck Risberg," I said. "I need you to sign out a revolver for me."

Bernhard looked like he didn't believe his own ears.

"What is going on?" he asked, when he'd composed himself.

"I need it."

"Kristian. What's going on?"

"Nothing, apart from I need it and you have to get it for me."

He looked me up and down.

"And how do you think I'll manage to do that?"

"You'll figure something out," I said.

"This is nuts, you're aware of that? Have you lost it completely?"

"The less you know the better," I said.

"You reek of booze," Bernhard said.

"Oh, shut up!"

"Go home. Forget about whatever it is you're planning to do."

"For Christ's sake, come on!"

"I'm not doing it. I don't want to get involved in this. You can find someone else to do it for you."

"Listen, Bernhard. I don't give a shit how far I have to go. I need the revolver and that's the end of it."

I hesitated for a moment, then I said: "If you don't help me I'll go to Risberg and tell him about Kaczorowski."

It looked like the features on his face lost all connection with one another.

"I couldn't give a fuck about it coming to light," I said. "I think you do, but I don't. I'll call him right now, if need be."

I took my mobile from my pocket.

"Jesus, Kristian, you're some fucking bastard."

I couldn't help but laugh.

"I know, Bernhard. I am. We both are. Two fucking bastards. Two absolute assholes."

Bernhard narrowed his eyes.

"So," I said, "are you going to sign it out or what?"

Maltek was irritable, obviously dissatisfied with something the three men were in the process of explaining to him as I made it to the top of the stairs, I'd heard raised voices above the beating of the rain and my presence among the dejected gathering didn't serve to lessen his displeasure. He growled something in greeting and looked in turn at each of the other three, as though expecting one of them to pipe up and inquire as to the purpose of my visit. I thought I recognized one of them, he was well dressed, perhaps I'd seen him in a courtroom, there was something in his self-assured expression that told me he was a lawyer. The smaller of the other two had feminine features, offset by an underbite. The last guy stood with one hand in his pocket but with his arm straight, making it look uncommonly short, as if everything from the elbow down was stuffed down his trousers.

"Inspector," Maltek said, finally. "What can I do for you today?"

He tried to adopt a different tone, but his voice was husky

and without inflection, like someone who'd just woken up, bearing no trace of the hysterical falsetto from last time.

"I'd like to have a word with you in private," I said, aware of the concentration required of me to enunciate the words, the alcohol in my system catching up with me all of a sudden, momentarily making me feel like I was about to pass out, there was a tightening behind my eyes and I felt a sharp pain at the base of my spine, the barrel of the revolver against my coccyx. I thought about taking it out, firing a warning shot at the wall, or better still, putting a bullet through the glass roof he was so proud of, and standing there with his cronies, all of them crestfallen, under a shower of glass and water. And I thought about what Maltek's bodyguard said to me on my first visit, that he was dangerous, and that I should watch myself, something I had yet to verify. But perhaps he just behaved himself in front of me? Because he was the one I'd seen with the teenage boy at Gunerius's place that day?

Maltek gestured towards the guy in the suit.

"Gudmundsson. My lawyer. And this is . . ." He looked at the two others. "Ah, never mind! There's nothing you can say to me that they can't hear."

"All the same, I have to insist," I said.

Maltek pulled a long face. Not much remained of the imperious show-off from last time, he sat slumped in the seat, brows knitted, looking as dejected as a man can be.

Then he glanced up at his associates.

"Go on down to the reception and get yourselves something to drink. I'll join you in a bit."

He stood up behind the desk.

"What about you, Inspector? Would you like anything?"

He looked me up and down, like Bernhard had done.

"Or have you had enough?"

He began to laugh but it ended up as more of a short grunt. The lawyer chuckled. The guy with the shriveled arm kept his eyes fixed on me on his way out. As soon as they closed the door behind them they started talking.

"How are things?" Maltek asked, his tone of voice already lighter, as though his problems had disappeared out the door with the others. "I've given a lot of thought to what we talked about last time."

I had no idea what he was referring to, but nodded all the same, I was unsteady, had to make a real effort to keep my balance, the back of my neck felt frail, like a bunch of twigs.

"You've no doubt been busy making inquiries, I suppose," he continued, I could feel his eyes on me, weighing me up, as if his chatter was simply a cover for the examination he was in reality subjecting me to. "And people have probably told you all kinds of strange things. But I could tell you a lot of strange things about them, as well. But I won't. Take note of that. I don't talk shit about other people. Why? Because I don't need to. Why would I? I have enough to be getting on with. And so should they. You are aware that almost everything we say about other people, no matter who they are, has its roots in jealousy? The reason we talk about other people at all is jealousy. Envy. There have been studies carried out on it, I know what I'm talking about. Remember that the next time someone gives you the lowdown on me. They're doing it because they're jealous. They're doing it because they want things to take a turn for me, for me to land in trouble, there's nothing that would please them more than to see everything I have go to the dogs. Me, I'm above that kind of thing. I have no scores to settle. I have enough things to get on with. And other people can get on with theirs, as long as they don't put a spoke in my wheel."

He was studying me carefully the whole time.

"Of course you can get a real itch to give someone a good fucking working over. I'm sure you get the urge to do the same sometimes, am I right? But that's exactly what separates us from the others. That's where the line goes, between those who manage to hold back and those who don't. Wouldn't you agree?"

I tried to swallow a lump I could feel in my throat and suddenly belched.

Maltek pretended not to notice.

"My first Norwegian hooker," he said, making a kissing sound with his lips. "I thought I had come to paradise on earth. Sheer cleanliness and virtue. No need for a condom. Just a quick wash. Turned out she had the worst thing going, after AIDS!"

He laughed: "I might as well have fucked an open wound!"

For a few moments it looked like his features were about to be overcome by anger.

Then he brightened up again: "But do I bear a grudge against her for it?" he said and smiled. "Not in the slightest! She helped increase my self-awareness. She made me see the big picture. I'm indebted to her."

His face took on a peculiar expression, of surprise, it seemed, at the fact that I wasn't as equally enthusiastic as him, now that he had regained inspiration.

"Some days you're unlucky, other days it's someone else. That's just the way it goes. That's how we balance one another. And I think it's pretty evenly distributed in the long run, don't you?"

The worst of the dizziness subsided, and with a little effort I managed to draw a deep enough breath to trust my voice would hold.

"My boss and I," I said, "we've agreed to content ourselves with one of you."

"Meaning?"

"Either you give us Gunerius."

"Give?" he mimicked.

"Or we pressure him until he gives you up. It's one out of two either way."

"Gunerius?" Maltek said. "The hotel baron, you mean? Don Gunerius?"

He flashed a broad smile.

"As you're aware, I hardly know the man. I've met him a couple of times, that's it."

"If that's how you want it."

"How am I supposed to give you Gunerius when I don't know him?"

"Okay. If that's the way it's going to be."

I made to leave.

"But I can give you something else," he hurried to say.

The drumming on the glass roof had ceased, a strange silence descended.

"You're together with a woman whose child is missing, right?"

He grinned, seeming to be uncertain of how far he could go.

Once again I felt dizziness take hold, as though what I had drunk had collected in one spot and had only now begun to circulate.

At first I thought of asking him what on earth he meant.

Instead I said: "What about it?"

Maltek made a face.

"I'm not sure," he said. "But there's a customer. One of the regulars. The Hen. Complete nut."

He giggled. The little girl's voice was back.

"He walks like this."

He pursed his lips, crossed his eyes and rocked his head back and forth.

The pout gave way to a new bout of laughter.

"He used to be in the shop every single day. Now it's been over a year since anyone's seen him."

The time span he specified sent a chill through me.

"And there are rumors."

He looked me up and down as he said it.

"They say he has a girl tied up at his place. Has had for a long time. And that's why he's not out much anymore."

He had the facial expression of someone or other I'd seen in a cartoon ages ago.

"That's all I know."

"Name and address," I said, feeling simultaneously woozy and lucid.

"It is quite . . ." he started to say, but his protests were somewhat halfhearted, and I only needed to repeat myself once more, in a calm, measured tone, for him to open a drawer in his desk and rummage around.

"I suppose things don't always go the way we've planned," he mumbled.

He looked up: "Ever read Asterix?"

He continued to root around.

"Asterix and Obelix are on their way to a Roman fort to make inquiries about a foundling. And it's important to Asterix that this be done with a certain tactfulness, since it's a delicate matter, so as they approach the fort, he makes clear to Obelix that he needs to remember that this has to be carried out with discretion. Obelix is slightly perplexed at having the prospect of a good punch-up taken away from him. But as it turns out, Asterix is the one who loses his temper and hey presto, the whole garrison is reduced to rubble. And as they're leaving, Obelix walks alongside Asterix looking at him delightedly, until eventually he says: I like your idea of discretion!"

His body began to shake.

"Here," he said, laughing so hard he struggled to catch his breath, as he took a notebook from the drawer, tore out a page, and wrote something on it.

"Pop by the reception and have yourself a drink on the way out," he said, thrusting the note into my hand.

"Hey!" he called out as I was halfway out the door, as if it annoyed him, my obtaining the information so easily, or was it an attempt to delay me and give the Hen the opportunity to slip away?

I turned around.

"You haven't answered my question!"

"Which question?"

"What the Holocaust was to Hitler!"

He grinned.

"A cry for help," I replied.

At first he just stared, dumbfounded at my knowing the answer. Then a simmering chuckle changed to shrill, girlish gasps before bubbling into hysterical laughter, and he held his arm around his stomach and doubled up.

"Fantastic!" he managed to utter. "A cry for help! Ha ha! Fantastic!"

I left. A warm breeze, the back sweep of air that arose as I opened the door, blew in my face. It smelled of wet pavement, the smell that comes when the heavens have emptied. I could still hear Maltek from inside. It sounded like clucking, as though I could already hear the guy I was on my way to see.

Something happened while I was driving out of the city center. A diffuse light appeared in the sky. The clouds became translucent at first, then disappeared, and a steel-gray vault became visible. It was the sky: nothing between it and the houses on the outskirts of the city. The further I drove, the brighter it became, as though I was nearing the very source of the light. After a half hour I left the freeway and turned on to a local road. I allowed myself a few proper swigs from the bottle. The brandy tore at my stomach, but offset the effect of what I'd already drunk: my head cleared, my hands gripped the wheel tighter, and the tiredness evaporated. The landscape leveled out and there were fewer cars on the road. Some red barns appeared. In the fields it looked like a battle had just been fought. A few scattered houses, swing sets and blue trampolines, before a big housing estate with homes arranged by color. At a large intersection I took a right turn, passing an inn and then driving along a tree-lined avenue. I went by more fields and farms, before new rows of houses appeared. The destination on the GPS indicated a point in the middle of a sharp curve in the road, where there was a two-story house with a large garden, which looked like it had once been well kept but was now covered in long dark grass. Short bright-green pine trees were growing all over. I parked in front of the garage, which was at road level. A fly crawled out of one of the dashboard vents and began butting the windshield with furious clicks. The house looked deserted, no lights, no clutter outside, nothing to suggest any life. I downed the rest of the bottle and moved the revolver to my jacket pocket before getting out: it seemed like I should find a use for it after having gone to all the trouble of getting it.

A narrow door, halfway along a white-walled ground floor,

led to what I assumed was a separate apartment. The second floor, covered in brown wood paneling, had a large, covered veranda. The blinds were drawn on both windows of the basement apartment. I rang twice but didn't hear anything, not even the doorbell. I put my hand to the door. It was locked. I made my way around the corner and up a decaying flight of steps leading to the back of the house. A flagpole stood up a slope in the corner of the garden, the line plinking. Something gave the place a maritime look: the window by the front door was small and round, like a porthole.

This time I heard sounds from inside as soon as I rang.

The door was opened. A short bespectacled man stood in the hall. What little hair he had was in a wreath from ear to ear, his bald crown shone, but he looked young all the same, like an actor who'd been made up to look old. He was wearing blue shorts and a white T-shirt, his eyes downcast. I waited for him to look up but his eyes were fixed on the floor.

"Vidar Sande?" I asked.

"Yes," he replied, without looking up.

He spoke so quietly, in such a frail tone, that I just about made out what he said.

I held up my badge. The movement obliged him to glance up. I caught a glimpse of his eyes, pale blue. Then he checked himself. With eyes once again downcast, he began nodding his head, as though something spring-loaded had been set off.

"Can I come in?" I asked.

He stood nodding for a long time before answering.

"Yes," he said, so faintly and feebly that it was like I'd just bawled him out.

He turned and walked back down the hall, still nodding. Maltek was right, I thought: like a hen. I entered and closed the door behind me. His flip-flops smacked against the flooring. We ended up in a kitchen that didn't look like it had ever been used. There was a pungent smell in there, like someone had just broken wind. Sande sat down at a round table with a little doily on it.

"You live here alone?" I asked.

"Yes," he said, his eyes had found a new spot on the floor to focus on.

"You're a customer of Jarosz Maltek," I said.

To my surprise, he glanced up when he replied, but without meeting my eyes.

"Yes," he said, beginning to nod again.

"What is it you buy at Maltek's?"

He got a strange look on his face, a mischievous flash, like a kid who wants a secret wrested from him.

"Porn?"

He tittered.

"What kind?" I asked.

He waited a moment, then said: "What do you mean?"

"What kind?" I repeated. "Boys or girls? Kiddies or grown-ups?"

"Different sorts," he said, "different sorts of stuff."

"Can I see some of it?"

"What . . . ?" He hesitated. "What is this all about? Honestly?" he added, and chuckled, uncertain as to whether he also had the right to ask questions. I looked at him. His age was completely indeterminate, somewhere between thirty and sixty. His arms were pale, his skin had something rubbery about it. The taste of cognac rose up into my mouth. I had a sudden feeling of nausea. It was as though I were drawing something inside for each breath I took, something that had previously been in him.

"What's on the first floor?"

He didn't reply.

"Is it an apartment?"

"Yes."

"Is someone living there?"

He laughed. "No."

"Can I take a look?"

He brought his hand to his mouth and began picking his teeth with the nail on his little finger. It was hard to imagine any food ever having been prepared in the house. I went back into the hall, looked around and caught sight of a door to the left of the entrance with a poster of Ole Gunnar Solskjær on it. I heard Sande behind me, but just as he was about to go past me, I swung my arm round and made contact. He hit the wall with a thud. Then we stood there, facing each other. He scratched his elbow. I could tell by looking at him he wouldn't try his luck a second time.

"You lead the way," I said, after a while.

He went over and opened the door. I followed after but very nearly fell headfirst as I began descending the staircase, and had to use the banisters to regain my balance.

The room we came down into seemed like a living room and had very few furnishings. There was a white sofa, a coffee table, a few empty bookshelves, a large TV, and a video game console. DVDs and games lay strewn on the floor. Both windows were covered with large foam rubber slabs, perfectly cut to fit the frames, and a congealed, transparent material bulged out all along the length of the molding and baseboards, silicon most likely.

"Who uses this room?" I asked.

"Me," he said, and tried to laugh, but all that came out was a whistling sound.

I picked up one of the magazines on the coffee table, a pop magazine for girls.

"You're reading this?"

He didn't say anything, just stood scratching his elbow and bobbing his head up and down. I felt bad for him. He seemed to be ashamed, dismayed that someone had seen the disgusting nest he had down there, which nobody else was ever supposed to know about.

A fresh surge of brandy flared in my throat. The magazine slipped from my hand and hit the floor with a smack. I felt like I could throw up at any second.

"Where is she?" I asked.

As though that was all he'd been waiting for, he put his hand in his pocket and produced a set of keys. I walked behind him as he made his way towards a white door. A sense of foreboding made me take the revolver from my jacket while he fiddled with the key in the lock, the weight of it in my hand was welcome and the nausea and light-headedness diminished slightly. Sande gestured for me to go first. I pointed the barrel at the door. He looked at the weapon but didn't say anything.

There was a rank smell of urine in the room. The ceiling and walls were covered with egg cartons that had been flattened and stapled together, as was one big window. Piles of clothes lay around the floor, along with some paper cups and plates with food remains on them. There were two unopened packs of diapers against one wall. Music was coming from a small TV propped on a stool.

Maria was sitting on a bed beneath the window. She was wearing nothing but pajama bottoms. She didn't look up when we entered, didn't take her eyes from the screen.

I walked over to her. She had a rope tied to one ankle, the end secured to the bedpost.

"Maria?" I said, and placed my hand on her head. But she took no notice, didn't react to my touch and seemed unaware of my presence.

I stroked her cheek, placed my hand gently on her chin and turned her head to face me. But the gaze that met mine was empty, her eyes sunk within each hollow, as if they didn't belong to anyone.

"Maria?" I said. "Can you hear me?"

No reaction at all. When I let go of her chin her head pivoted back around.

"What the fuck have you done to her?" I said.

I heard hurried footsteps. When I turned, Sande was already halfway out the door. I raced after him, got hold of his T-shirt and pulled him back into room. Then I pistol-whipped him across the mouth. His lip split, a thin jet of blood shooting out. He stumbled backwards. His glasses fell off. Then he dropped to the floor.

I looked over at Maria, she'd turned around and sat looking at us. But it was like she wasn't there, like what had been her had left, that only the husk remained. I thought about the entire year she had spent there. The days passing, the Hen going about his daily business upstairs, Maria down below, locked in her room, the evenings he sat watching TV, perhaps forgetting at times that she even existed, that she was there, right below him. How often did he think of her? How often did he go down to her? What did he do to her when he did? Was he ashamed afterwards? Or did he just eagerly await his next visit? Did they talk? Or did he have her doped up the whole time? How long did he think he could keep her? Was there ever any regret on his part, did he ever consider letting her go? Or did nothing challenge his resolve to stick firmly to the plan he'd worked out? How much thought had gone into it? Had he devised everything, down to the very last detail, or had he simply stumbled upon her that night in April, the demented idea occurring right there and then and proving irresistible? It had been raining that night: had he offered her a ride home? How long had it taken before she realized his true intentions? Had she lain in the back screaming? Or was she already drugged? Had he raped her as soon as they got to the house or had he waited, held back, bided his time and looked forward to it long before he made his first move?

The sun must have broken through the clouds, gleaming rays of white light shone through the cracks in the stapled egg cartons. Maria's features fell into darkness, the outline of her head

glowed. Nothing in this world can bring her back, I thought.
Nobody will manage to wake her. Nothing can be heard above
the silence that has descended within her. She doesn't belong
here anymore. She's living in another world. I'm too late after
all. She's gone for good.

Sande was sitting on the floor with his hands over his mouth.
He was crying. I walked over and gave him a kick.

"Up!"

He got up quickly, his glasses making a crunching sound
under his feet. His top lip had swollen to a dark bulge. Tears
ran down his face. I shoved him against the wall and jammed
the end of the barrel under his split lip.

"Okay, you piece of shit. Are you listening to me?"

I hit him across the face.

"Are you listening to me?"

He nodded, still dazed.

I struck him again.

"I can't hear you."

"Yes," he peeped. His fat lip distorted his voice. A dark-red
streak ran from his mouth as he spoke: "Yes, I'm listening."

I looked over my shoulder. Maria had crawled up onto the
bed, moving in a daze on all fours, her hair hung down over her
face, she resembled a sick animal, there was a large, dark stain
on the back of her pajama bottoms.

I pressed my forearm against Sande's chest and applied
pressure.

"All right, you fucker," I said.

There was a mooing sound from behind me, I turned, a thin
string of vomit hung from Maria's mouth. Then more lowing.
Her back arched. The thin string became a thicker jet.

"You're going to get an offer," I whispered, putting the
revolver to Sande's temple. "I'm going to make you an offer. Do
you understand?"

He opened his mouth but all that came out was more of the

dark-red discharge. My tongue bulged, feeling like a fillet of meat, and something rose up in my throat and pressed against my larynx.

I hit him.

"I can't hear you."

"Yes," he bleated.

"I'm going to make you an offer. I'm giving you a chance. If you do as I say. If you do what I say, then you can walk away from this. You understand?"

This time he answered straight away, terrified of being struck again.

"Yes, I understand."

"What is it you understand?" I roared.

"That . . . that . . . that if I do exactly as you say, then I'll get another chance."

"The slightest fuck up," I said, "and you'll wind up with your teeth knocked in sucking cock for the rest of your life."

I pressed the revolver hard against his nose until I heard a snap.

He let out a scream.

"I understand," he said, with a lisp. "I understand what you're saying."

Light flooded into the room behind me, as though day were breaking for the first time.

"What is it you want me to do?" Sande said in a nasal tone.

I suddenly realized the reek of his breath was the same stench as in the kitchen. I turned away. Over on the bed, Maria had begun pulling the egg cartons off the window, she was on all fours, squinting confusedly into the harsh light.

"What is it you want me to do?"

Golden clouds puffed up here and there as I drove back towards the city. The clipped arc of a rainbow rose from the roof of a petrol station. Drivers and their passengers coming in the opposite direction gaped upwards. It looked like an enormous roof over our heads had been ripped off.

I parked in the burned-out ruins and walked the rest of the way. The pavement shone, the reflected light blinding no matter where you looked. I rang the buzzer, careful not to hold in the button too long. It was a while before she answered.

"Inger," I said, "it's me. Kristian. I need to talk to you. It's important. Please."

She hesitated for a moment. Just the sound of static over the intercom. Then the muffled crackle of the lock.

I raced up the stairs. I had a horrible feeling she wouldn't be there if I didn't move fast enough. Her door on the third floor was ajar. I could see her through the gap, standing in the hall, at a little distance from the entrance. The door snagged when I tried to open it, a brass chain preventing it from swinging open. Inger stood looking at me. She seemed frightened, as though afraid I'd enter by force.

"Please," I said. "Please open up."

I put my entire weight against the door, the strain on the chain between us making a grating sound.

"I need to talk to you."

Finally, she moved. She walked slowly over and unhooked the chain. Her face looked like it had the first time I'd been there. Then, as though to err on the side of caution, she returned to where she'd been standing. The door had swung open by itself in the meantime. I entered, but halted before I got too close, so as not to scare her. We stood facing each other. I was out of breath and had to wait a moment before I could speak.

"Inger," I said. "Dear, dear Inger, you have to listen to me."

My lungs were burning, I wasn't able to say any more.

Then she lifted her hand. I took it, and I don't know which one of us pulled the other close. We held each other. She began to cry. Then she surrendered completely, it was as though our bodies slipped smoothly into one form, and I felt, deep down, that I had finally made it, had finally arrived at something that I wanted to last, something that I couldn't face ever coming to an end.

Stig Sæterbakken (1966–2012) was one of Norway's most acclaimed contemporary writers. His novels include *Through the Night, Siamese, Self-Control,* and *Don't Leave Me* (all published by Dalkey Archive Press).

Seán Kinsella is from Dublin. He has translated four of Stig Sæterbakken's novels.